MW01028045

Saekisan
ILLUSTRATION BY
Hanekoto

©Hanekoto

"I'd just be happy to spend more time with you, Amane…"

©Hanekoto

Chitose Shirakawa

Itsuki Akazawa

©Hanekoto

Amane Fujimiya

Mahiru Shiina

"In my heart, I'm always by your side."

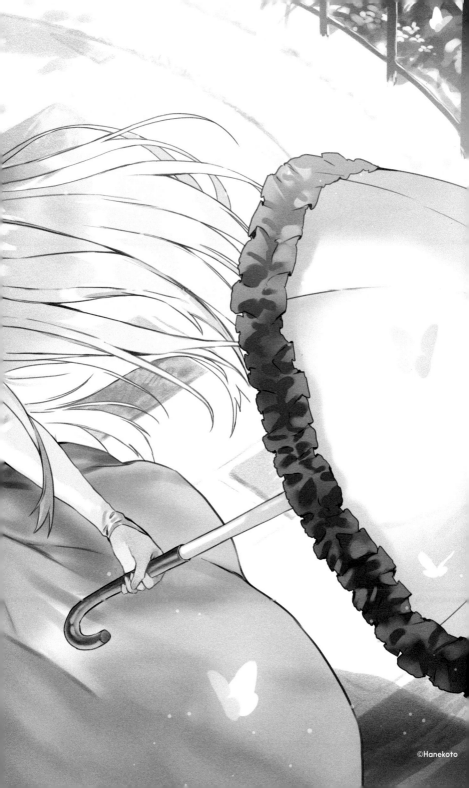

©Hanekoto

Contents

Chapter 1 The Angel Wakes Up 001

Chapter 2 Getting Drenched Was Worth It 027

Chapter 3 An Ideal Look 039

Chapter 4 A Stay-at-Home Date with the Angel 047

Chapter 5 One More Farewell 083

Chapter 6 The Angel and the Suspicious Figure 119

Chapter 7 A Summer Festival with the Angel 135

Chapter 8 Finish Your Homework First 183

Chapter 9 A Once-Desired, Now Undesired Meeting,
          and a Resolution 197

Amane Fujimiya

A student who began living alone when he
started high school. He's poor at every type of
housework and lives a slovenly life. Has a low
opinion of himself and tends to put himself
down, but is kind at heart.

Mahiru Shiina

A classmate who lives in the apartment next
door to Amane. The most beautiful girl in
school; everyone calls her an "angel." Started
cooking for Amane because she couldn't
overlook his unhealthy lifestyle.

©Hanekoto

The Angel Next Door Spoils Me Rotten

6

Saekisan

ILLUSTRATION BY
Hanekoto

NEW YORK

The Angel Next Door Spoils Me Rotten 6

Saekisan

TRANSLATION BY NICOLE WILDER ✳ COVER ART BY HANEKOTO

This book is a work of fiction. Names, characters, places, and incidents are the product of the author's imagination or are used fictitiously. Any resemblance to actual events, locales, or persons, living or dead, is coincidental.

OTONARI NO TENSHISAMA NI ITSUNOMANIKA DAMENINGEN NI SARETEITA KEN Vol. 6
Copyright © 2022 Saekisan
Illustration © 2022 Hanekoto
All rights reserved.
Original Japanese edition published in 2022 by SB Creative Corp.
This English edition is published by arrangement with SB Creative Corp., Tokyo in care of Tuttle-Mori Agency, Inc., Tokyo.

English translation © 2024 by Yen Press, LLC

Yen Press, LLC supports the right to free expression and the value of copyright. The purpose of copyright is to encourage writers and artists to produce the creative works that enrich our culture.

The scanning, uploading, and distribution of this book without permission is a theft of the author's intellectual property. If you would like permission to use material from the book (other than for review purposes), please contact the publisher. Thank you for your support of the author's rights.

Yen On
150 West 30th Street, 19th Floor
New York, NY 10001

Visit us at yenpress.com ✳ facebook.com/yenpress ✳ twitter.com/yenpress
yenpress.tumblr.com ✳ instagram.com/yenpress

First Yen On Edition: January 2024
Edited by Yen On Editorial: Emma McClain, Ivan Liang
Designed by Yen Press Design: Liz Parlett

Yen On is an imprint of Yen Press, LLC.
The Yen On name and logo are trademarks of Yen Press, LLC.

The publisher is not responsible for websites (or their content) that are not owned by the publisher.

Library of Congress Cataloging-in-Publication Data
Names: Saekisan, author. | Hanekoto, illustrator. | Wilder, Nicole. translator.
Title: The angel next door spoils me rotten / Saekisan ; illustration by Hanekoto ; translation by Nicole Wilder.
Other titles: Otonari no tenshi-sama ni Itsu no ma ni ka dame ningen ni sareteita ken. English
Description: First Yen On edition. | New York : Yen On, 2020– |
Identifiers: LCCN 2020043583 | ISBN 9781975319236 (v. 1 ; trade paperback) |
ISBN 9781975322694 (v. 2 ; trade paperback) |
ISBN 9781975333409 (v. 3 ; trade paperback) |
ISBN 9781975344405 (v. 4 ; trade paperback) |
ISBN 9781975348274 (v. 5 ; trade paperback) |
ISBN 9781975372569 (v. 5.5 ; trade paperback) |
ISBN 9781975372583 (v. 6 ; trade paperback)
Subjects: CYAC: Love—Fiction.
Classification: LCC PZ7.1.S2413 An 2020 | DDC [Fic]—dc23
LC record available at https://lccn.loc.gov/2020043583

ISBNs: 978-1-9753-7258-3 (paperback)
978-1-9753-7259-0 (ebook)

10 9 8 7 6 5 4 3 2 1

LSC-C

Printed in the United States of America

Chapter 1

The Angel Wakes Up

He could hear the chirping of birds coming from somewhere.

Amane's thoughts gradually came into focus as his mind slowly left the comfortable languidness and warmth of slumber. Somehow, he managed to open his heavy eyelids and resisted the temptation to go back to sleep.

As he became more aware of the world, still blurry, Amane realized that the morning sun was streaming in through the open curtains, and there was a source of warmth beside him that wasn't usually there.

He felt its heat slowly seeping into him, perhaps because the timer on the air conditioner had run out. But the feeling wasn't unpleasant.

Without pausing to worry about the fatigue that still permeated his body, he embraced that bundle of warmth and was met with a gentle, sweet aroma and a hoarse little groan that sounded just as sweet.

"Nnh."

When he finally took a good look, Amane's view was filled with an enchanting river of gold, something he wasn't accustomed to seeing upon waking.

Amane swallowed the exclamation rising in his throat at the sight of Mahiru sleeping peacefully in his arms and sighed deeply instead. He was relieved he had managed to keep quiet.

…That's right, yesterday I fell asleep with Mahiru.

He remembered what had happened, so he didn't leap up in shock, but the memory didn't ease the burden that this placed upon his waking heart.

He felt the heavy *thump, thump* of the pounding inside his chest, but when he looked at Mahiru's peaceful, sleeping face, little by little, his heartbeat regained its normal calm rhythm.

Inhaling deeply to compose himself, he gazed again at Mahiru.

She was breathing regularly in her sleep with her head resting on Amane's upper arm. Mahiru looked so lovely that he was completely mesmerized by the sight of her.

She must have felt utterly safe because her cheeks had relaxed into a happy expression, giving the impression that she wore a gentle smile even in her sleep.

…She looks so unguarded and adorable.

It would be no exaggeration to say she had the face of a sleeping angel. She seemed so beautiful and pure, just like her nickname.

If he said that to her face, she would likely get embarrassed and sulk for a while, but as long as he kept the thought to himself, he could mull it over as much as he liked.

Though, if I whispered it now, she probably wouldn't notice.

As he gazed at her, transfixed by how cute she was, he tenderly stroked Mahiru's head with his free hand.

As he combed his fingers gently through her immaculate, silky hair—her angel's halo—he carefully shifted to change his position ever so slightly, doing his best not to lift his numb arm that she was using in place of a pillow. His new position afforded him a better view of Mahiru's sleeping face.

The tingling in his arm was a small price to pay.

Smiling softly at Mahiru, who still showed no signs of waking, he stroked her cushiony-looking cheek with his fingertip. As he watched her tirelessly, the sound of knocking came from his door.

"Amane, you awake?"

It was his father, speaking casually to him from the other side of the door.

I wonder what he wants.

Amane's father had probably come to wake him up, but if Amane replied now, he might rouse Mahiru.

It would be a pity to disturb her when she was sleeping so peacefully, and personally, Amane wanted to watch her like this for a little longer.

However, if he didn't answer, his father might come in, so he wasn't sure what to do. But before he could come up with a plan, the door opened.

He saw his father's familiar figure, and Amane's face stiffened in a grimace.

When his father looked toward the bed, however, his eyes went wide and he put on a little smile, saying, "Oh!"

Amane instantly sensed that his father was going to tell his mother, Shihoko, about this and that he would undoubtedly be teased for it later. His face twitched as he resigned himself to the humiliation. He then held up his index finger in front of his mouth.

He didn't make a shushing sound, but he hoped that his father would understand what he meant.

His father, who was always quick to catch on, nodded in response to Amane's gesture. He took one last amused look at his son, then waved and quietly left the room.

Amane listened to the sound of the door fittings sliding gently together and his father's restrained, receding footsteps. After they had faded, Amane let out a silent sigh.

I hope he doesn't get the wrong idea…

The sight of a couple sleeping in bed together was sure to invite misunderstandings.

Although they were dating, and it was true they had spent the night in his room together like this, they had an extremely wholesome relationship and had only ever kissed and held hands. But Amane's parents had no way of knowing how far they had taken things.

Actually, since there were no signs that anything had happened, his father probably wasn't all that suspicious. Even so, it was embarrassing to be caught like this.

As Amane prepared himself to be questioned later, he stroked Mahiru's hair, and the delicate girl in his arms stirred slightly.

It was probably rare for Mahiru, who kept a very regular schedule, to sleep in so late.

"…Nnh."

She made a little sound in her throat and buried her face back into Amane's chest as if seeking warmth. As much as he loved her, he knew that if he obeyed his urges and held her close, she would wake completely, so he held back and only stroked her head.

He was sure that the air conditioner had already turned off, but Mahiru did not pull away from him; instead, she nuzzled her cheek into his chest. He wondered if she got cold easily. When he touched her toes with his own, he could tell that she ran cooler than him, so he figured his guess was probably right.

In that case, the AC last night must have been a little chilly.

Feeling guilty, he wrapped his legs around Mahiru's to warm her up and gently put his free arm around her back to better share his body heat.

As they basked in each other's warmth, a happy feeling filled him. When he cradled her soft body and touched her gently, however, she stirred more than before and slowly turned her head to look in his direction.

Her caramel-colored eyes were still unfocused as they took in Amane's face. They looked so rich and dewy that he could almost hear the drip of crystal-clear water.

Her expression was somewhat slack, and she looked incredibly childish.

"Sorry, did I wake you?" he asked.

When he smiled at the drowsy-looking Mahiru and stroked her head again, she closed her eyes softly and let herself fall back into his arms.

She's still half asleep, he realized. But she was also half awake, and when he ran his finger affectionately down Mahiru's cheek, she let out a highly adorable groan.

...Mahiru's kind of needy when she's getting up, huh?

She was so charming that Amane couldn't help but gaze at her and touch her affectionately. As expected, however, after about five minutes of that, she became fully aware of the world, and her eyes snapped open.

Once he was certain she was really awake, Amane said good morning and planted a deliberate kiss on Mahiru's cheek.

When he did, he got to enjoy seeing Mahiru grow suddenly stiff.

"...Ah, Amane...? Wh-why—?"

"You don't remember? After we spent such a hot night together?"

He could tell she hadn't completely grasped the situation yet, so he playfully worded his question in a misleading way.

Incidentally, he wasn't lying. While it hadn't been a night of passion, it had been quite warm, temperature-wise. He decided to keep the fact that the AC had been cooling them off to himself for the moment.

When she heard that they had spent the night together, Mahiru looked at Amane and squeaked out "H-huh?" then checked her appearance.

Her clothes might have been a little bit disheveled, but he was sure there were absolutely no signs they had done anything indecent. It would be a real problem if there were, since nothing had actually happened.

"Just joking... We didn't do anything."

"R-right..."

"Well, I did kiss you on the cheek and stuff. Just now."

He laughed and said that surely a good morning kiss was permissible, and Mahiru flushed bright red. She mumbled quietly, "This is too much excitement first thing in the morning." So he kept his laughter hushed.

"...It looked like you felt totally safe while you were lying there. How'd you sleep?" Amane asked as he helped Mahiru sit up. She seemed to be completely awake at last.

Wrapped in his embrace, Mahiru cast her eyes downward in apparent embarrassment. "...I, um, felt really calm in your arms."

"Your heart doesn't race?"

"I-it does, but...but I'm calm."

She mumbled that it was racing now and wrapped her arms around Amane's back. Amane chuckled and peered into her face.

"If it calms you down, we could sleep together every night."

"Th-that's, um—"

"Still joking."

He'd made the suggestion knowing that Mahiru would get flustered, so he didn't particularly mind when she didn't take him up on it.

For Amane's part, he was afraid that if they somehow ended up sleeping together every night, it would drive him crazy. For the moment, he was doing a fairly good job of holding back when his heart began to pound, but if they started sleeping beside each other regularly, he was afraid that sooner or later he would be unable to resist making a move.

Having persuaded himself that since he couldn't trust his reason to save him, he had to dismiss the suggestion as a joke, Amane noticed that Mahiru was hanging her head.

Wondering if he had teased her too much, he patted her back lightly to comfort her. She lifted her face to look up at him, and he saw that her cheeks were flushed a rosy pink.

"...M-maybe, every once in a while...," she muttered in a quiet, squeaky voice.

Amane's mind went blank for a second.

Every once in a while.

In other words, she didn't mind the idea of staying over. She liked sleeping by his side.

"Are you saying that seriously?" he asked.

"If we're d-dating, then spending the night...should be okay, shouldn't it?"

"...S-sure, I guess so."

When she put it like that, he couldn't argue.

After all, it was normal for high school couples to spend the night together. In fact, Amane and Mahiru were probably moving at an exceptionally slow pace.

Itsuki often stayed over at Chitose's place, and the two of them were fine with doing things still a long way off for Amane and Mahiru.

The problem was that if Mahiru said she was staying over, Amane knew that he would expect those sorts of things, even if only just a little. It was in his nature as a man; and as her boyfriend, he couldn't help but have certain expectations.

Mahiru seemed to guess what Amane was thinking. She panicked, her face somehow turning even more red, and she looked at Amane through slightly teary eyes.

"That's— I didn't— I'm not hoping for that sort of thing, or any-thing… I'd just be happy to spend more time with you, Amane…"

"…Uh-huh."

"…Is that…bad?"

"Of course not. I'm glad to hear it."

Mahiru looked up at him uneasily. As Amane firmly reassured her, a little of his true feelings came through.

Mahiru was trembling with embarrassment. Feeling guilty, Amane swallowed the urges rising in him and stroked her head.

"…W-well, another time, yeah?"

"Y-yes."

"Come on, we ought to hurry up and get dressed. You're going to change, right?"

"R-right, yes."

He decided to table their discussion for the time being. If they gave it any further thought, it was likely to derail the whole day.

As Amane took a deep breath and tried to regain his composure, he pulled away from Mahiru, who, perhaps out of bashfulness, sprang out of bed, then turned to look back at him.

As he was wondering what might be the matter, all of a sudden, the distance between them closed.

He smelled her light, sweet fragrance and felt something soft against his lips.

Both sensations vanished as fast as they came, and in their place, gently fluttering flaxen hair tickled his cheek.

"You teased me a lot earlier, Amane, so I'm just paying you back."

She announced this with a bright-red face, as if braving her embarrassment, then flipped her hair and quickly left the room.

Amane watched her go, then went to lie right back down on the bed.

I need to calm down before I can get back up.

Marveling at Mahiru's unexpected boldness, Amane continued staring at the ceiling until the heat left his body.

"Oh, Amane. Good morning."

His parents were already sitting in the dining room, waiting for him.

He could hear the sounds of cooking in the kitchen and caught a glimpse of familiar flaxen hair, so he knew Mahiru was making his omelet as promised.

"...Morning."

"Here, sit, sit," his mother said. "Mahiru is making breakfast for you right now."

"Great."

It had taken a while for Amane to return to earth, so he had arrived downstairs quite late. During that time, Mahiru must have come down ahead of him and started preparations.

She had promised earlier to make an omelet for him, so the timing had worked out perfectly. Going forward, however, he hoped she would tone down the flirting first thing in the morning.

"You two get on so well," his mother remarked.

"...I think that's pretty normal, if two people are dating."

"Well, that's certainly true, but you're well past just boyfriend and girlfriend, aren't you?" his father remarked. "You're more like newlyweds."

As Amane's father looked at his son and made this casual remark, there came a clattering sound from the kitchen, like someone dropping a plate into the sink.

Amane was relieved not to hear it break. He surmised that Mahiru had had a little accident out of shock.

"Oh no, Mahiru dear, are you all right?" his mother asked.

"Y-yes, and the plate isn't broken. I'm sorry I dropped it…"

"That's fine! Could have happened to anyone."

Amane was pretty sure it had been completely avoidable, but he didn't say a thing, and he chose to ignore his mother's gaze as she grinned at him.

He had learned over the past sixteen years that if he entertained her for even a moment, she would never let up.

His mother seemed disappointed that Amane didn't play along, but she obeyed when his father gently told her not to tease him, which gave Amane some peace of mind.

A little while later, breakfast was set out on the table. Once Mahiru finished Amane's omelet and took her seat, the four of them began to eat.

"So I take it that something happened yesterday while we were out?"

But no sooner had Amane taken a big bite of rice than his mother sent a pointed question flying right at him, and he froze.

He had been sure he would be asked about spending the night with Mahiru, but his mother, sensing that there had been a precipitating event, had asked about that instead. That took him by surprise.

His mouth was full, so Amane had a moment as he chewed and swallowed before he had to answer.

"…What makes you think that?" he asked.

"Because you seemed different when we got back," his mother replied. "It would be stranger if nothing had happened at all."

"Of course we can tell when something's different about our own son," his father added. "Don't underestimate your parents, now."

Amane thought he had been acting normally, but apparently his mother and father had seen right through him.

They were looking at him anxiously, but as far as Amane was concerned, the matter was over. He had already gotten past it, so there was no reason for them to worry.

"It's nothing, really. When we went for a walk, we ran into Tou-jou, and he had some things to say, that's all."

"Ah, so that's what it was… The way you're acting, it seems like you're already over it."

"I guess I am. Or rather, I've overcome it. I don't think he's going to bother me anymore."

When Amane thought back to that time in his life, his chest no longer hurt. Though he had run into the very person who might be called the ringleader, he had remained calm.

As he thought about it again, he was keenly reminded that his calm reaction had been thanks to Mahiru, who had been sitting by his side.

"You've grown, haven't you? That's great."

His father seemed relieved.

Amane had caused his parents a great deal of worry at the time, and they were still anxious, even now. He had more or less regained his footing in high school, but it seemed their worry had never disappeared.

His father might be reassured, but his mother looked exasperated when she heard Toujou's name.

"I haven't had a chance to see the Toujous lately, but their son doesn't seem to have changed one bit," she said. "His parents are such nice people, too. I wonder if he's still in his rebellious phase."

Because of her job and personality, Amane's mother had a ridiculously large circle of acquaintances. He didn't know and probably couldn't even imagine how well-connected she was.

Of course, she was friends with people in town and had some connection to Toujou's parents as well.

Amane had also met Toujou's parents before, and he remembered them as extremely nice, straightforward people. They had even apologized to him for their son's actions, and he didn't hold anything against them.

"Who knows?" said Amane. "We don't have any real relationship, and I don't really care either way. I don't expect I'll see him very often anymore."

"The way you're able to make a clean break like that is one of your strong points, Amane," his father remarked. "...If seeing him had been stressful for you, I would have regretted asking you to come home."

Amane had promised to visit every six months, but it seemed his parents had been anxious about it and had hesitated to ask him to return.

"I'm the one who decided to come back... Besides, it turned out to be a good thing, seeing him. I was able to put it all behind me."

Amane was glad he had run into Toujou when he did.

He didn't think it was wrong to run away from things that were unbearably painful, if that was what it took to spare him.

And yet for Amane as he was now, confronting Toujou the day before had been the right thing to do.

Rather than continually running away from his past and letting the discomfort linger deep in his heart, it was better to overcome it head-on and turn it into a source of strength. And precisely because he had weathered such adversity, he'd attained a sound, sturdy core.

Thanks to Toujou and the other boys he hadn't seen for some time, Amane had been able to meet Mahiru. For that, he was actually eternally grateful to them. It would probably make them uncomfortable to hear it, but he was surprisingly thankful for their presence in his life.

When she saw that Amane was in no distress, his mother put on a tender smile. "All children really do grow up eventually, I suppose," she said. "Back then, you seemed so broken, and we were so worried. But...it seems like there's no need for that anymore."

"Love makes a person stronger, after all," his father added.

"Don't use such corny lines, Dad..."

"But it's true, isn't it?"

"...I guess so."

Amane had been able to make a strong recovery thanks to Mahiru, and now that he could stand on his own two feet, they could each support the other.

He was embarrassed to call this the power of love or anything like that, and he hadn't been able to say it out loud, but it was true that their relationship was the motivating force driving Amane.

"Ha-ha, I'm so glad you finally found a good partner. Like your mom is to me."

"...Y-yeah."

Mahiru, who had been listening silently to their conversation, had curled up in obvious embarrassment. Now Amane's parents turned their smiling gazes on her.

"You make sure to lean on Amane, too, Mahiru sweetheart," his mother said. "I worry about you, always looking after him."

"N-no, I... I'm always depending on Amane. He supports me all the time."

Amane felt like that was his line, but Mahiru was looking at him bashfully as if she truly felt that way.

"That's great... And, Amane, don't you take Mahiru's dedication for granted. Look out for each other, you hear?"

"Of course! We're always together, so obviously we're there for each other."

That wasn't something he needed to be told. That's exactly what he intended to do.

He didn't want to become the sort of person who did nothing but rely on their partner, never thinking about the burdens they placed on them.

Mahiru certainly spoiled Amane, but he didn't want to end up totally rotten.

Just as Mahiru had supported him this time, if she ever went through anything difficult, he would prop her up and hold her hand as they moved forward together.

That's what it meant to walk through life as a couple—a conviction that had been deeply etched into his heart as he'd watched his parents. Amane wished to be like them.

He felt certain that having found such a partner was the greatest happiness.

He wasn't going to walk by Mahiru's side with superficial resolve. When he looked over at her with that in mind, he saw that she was trembling, her face somehow even redder.

She appeared about to cry, but it would be more accurate to say that she looked ready to explode from embarrassment.

The moment she met Amane's gaze, she cast her eyes downward again. It was clear that she could barely stand the awkwardness.

Even so, there was no way he could let her go, and when he tried squeezing her hand under the table—after her whole body jumped from the shock of it—she squeezed his hand back.

"Oh my goodness, you're so cute! If I didn't have to go to work now, I would just smother you with love." His mother grinned at Mahiru.

Amane believed her. If she didn't have work, she probably would have spent the whole day doting on Mahiru.

"Hurry up and go to work already," said Amane.

"And you'll be here canoodling while we're gone, huh?"

"Yeah. Is that a problem?"

It seemed like his parents were going to make fun of him no matter what he said, so he boldly affirmed his mother's suspicions. The hand holding his trembled but didn't loosen its grip.

©Hanekoto

He wasn't sure, but he thought Mahiru must be happy.

Before, Amane would have totally denied everything, so his mother was surprised. She smiled happily.

"You're awfully defiant," she remarked.

"And you're awfully annoying," he replied.

"This is great. Spring has finally come for our Amane."

"I dunno; they seem pretty hot and heavy. Maybe it's already summer," his father added.

"Says two people who might as well be living in the tropics."

"As our child, you're definitely at risk of joining the club."

His mother actually seemed to be enjoying herself. She smiled at them as if giving her blessing. Amane shot her a sour look, but Mahiru didn't seem that put out, so he gave up and just looked away.

Amane's parents left to go to work, and the two teenagers ended up sitting side by side on Amane's bed.

It might have been because of where they were sitting, but even though there was as much distance between them as usual, Mahiru looked somewhat stiff, and it was obvious that she was extremely aware of Amane's presence.

She kept glancing over at him, and whenever their eyes met, she would blush slightly, making Amane feel a little embarrassed as well.

After a few minutes of repeatedly meeting his gaze and looking away, she asked timidly, "S-so canoodling?"

Apparently the word had been weighing on her mind, and after she said it out loud, her red cheeks grew even redder.

"Hmm? Oh, I said that to my parents so they wouldn't pry any more than necessary. I would have gotten teased if I'd denied it."

"Th-that seems likely, but…does that mean we're not really going to fool around…?"

"Well, I mean, I'd like to, personally."

What he'd said to his parents had mostly been for show, but as for Amane's feelings on the matter, he was eager to "canoodle" as much as Mahiru would permit.

Still, that sounded a little greedy even to him, and he almost laughed at himself for saying it.

But Mahiru consented, her voice weak, "...O-okay."

Though she nodded in agreement, she was squirming and shrinking, looking downright sheepish. Amane forced a smile, aware that her mind was running on overdrive.

"But if you don't want to, it's fine."

"That's not it. I'm not opposed to the idea. As long as it's with you, um, I'm open to any kind of...c-canoodling."

"Oh?"

"B-but um...specifically, what do we do to f-fool around?"

Silence fell over them in the wake of Mahiru's question.

Though he recalled having a similar conversation in the past, Amane was not sure what kind of answer he should give this time, and he fumbled for a moment.

"...Kissing and stuff."

"And stuff?"

"...You know, like...kissing?"

"So just kissing, then?"

"W-well, I'm not really sure how to answer that. There's, like, hugging and holding hands...which we always do, so—"

The two of them had been so close that they'd been flirting unconsciously since before they'd even started dating. But when it came to consciously fooling around, neither of them knew specifically what they should do.

Cuddling probably counted, and kissing did for sure, but Amane wasn't certain whether that was enough.

Fooling around more than that wasn't really something to do in one's parents' house, and Amane wanted to treasure Mahiru, so he had no intention of ruining everything over some momentary urges.

"What should we do in addition to the usual?" Mahiru wondered.

"...For now, we could cuddle?" he suggested.

This was nothing novel, and it was mild at best, but even so, his heart was pounding. His proposal earned a quiet "...Okay" in response.

Mahiru started to lean against him, hesitantly bringing her body closer to his, so Amane extended his hands to catch her...then smoothly slid his arms under her knees and around her back, picking her up. He was amused by her sweet high-pitched shriek as he moved her so she was sitting between his crossed legs on top of the bed.

"I prefer it like this."

"...S-sure."

"You don't like it?" he asked Mahiru, who was drawing her already dainty body in to be even smaller.

Mahiru shook her head slowly.

"Th-that's not it. I just...um, when we're like this, it's as if I'm being wrapped up by you, Amane...," she said sweetly.

"Do you want me to literally wrap you up?"

Amane folded his arms around Mahiru and hugged her tight. As soon as he did, her face went bright red, and she turned to look at him, faint tears in her eyes.

He wasn't in any position to talk, but he found it adorable how Mahiru got embarrassed so easily and blushed at the slightest things.

They had been dating for about two months, but they still weren't used to such close contact, and her inexperience was showing.

But the same was true for Amane. He didn't let it show on his face, but his heart was throbbing violently and wouldn't stop.

If Mahiru had put her ear to his body at that moment and listened, the pounding in his chest would have been obvious.

He was pretending to be totally calm, so it would be awkward if she found out how nervous he really was. Praying that she couldn't hear his heart beating, he pressed his lips against the back of Mahiru's head.

The feeling of his touch shouldn't have been a big deal, but it was enough to make Mahiru jolt and tremble. He could tell she was very nervous.

"…I'm just hugging you, you know."

"I—I know… My heart is pounding, but I'm happy… I like it when you squeeze me tight."

"You do? Then I'll do it as much as you like," he whispered close to her ear as he embraced her slim body. She shook conspicuously.

He laughed a little at how sensitive her ears were, then gently blew across one. Mahiru shook again and whirled around. Her eyes were blurry with tears, and he got the feeling that he had gone a little too far.

"…Amane!"

"Sorry, sorry, I didn't mean to."

"Y-you know I'm ticklish… That was mean." She pouted. "If you don't stop, I'll tell you something I heard about your past the other day."

"Uh-oh, I wouldn't like that."

He felt he might faint in agony if she whispered such things into his ear, so he took care not to tease Mahiru too much as he continued.

He didn't know how much he should touch her, or in what way, so he played it safe, stroking and squeezing her hands, and planting kisses on the back of her head, but as he had expected, that felt a little insufficient.

Though part of him was satisfied, another part of him seemed to disagree, protesting that it wasn't enough. He was able to keep it under control for the moment, but he didn't know when that part of him might act out, so he remained a little on edge.

He wanted to touch Mahiru more, to savor her softness.

But despite his wishes, his sense of decency would not allow him to go any further, so in the end, he limited himself to gentle touches.

But even that seemed to embarrass Mahiru, who couldn't keep her ears from flushing red.

She's really cute…

Even though Mahiru had initiated plenty of contact in the past, lately she was the one acting bashful. Before, Amane had been the nervous one, but now he could feel her embarrassment, as if their positions had reversed.

Amane squeezed her hand lightly, trying to suppress his desires, and Mahiru squeezed his back.

"…Amane, your hands are so big."

"Hmm? Well, I guess they might be a little large for my height."

Amane was tall, and on the whole, all the parts of his body were scaled to match. His feet were relatively large, and so were his hands. His palms were one or two sizes larger than Mahiru's, so when they held hands, the smallness of her frame was apparent.

"I like your hands… And I like it when you touch me."

"I'll touch you more if you say things like that."

Amane's sense of reason threatened to abandon its post at Mahiru's bold words. He wished she would be more prudent, but as if oblivious to his inner turmoil, she muttered quietly, "I wouldn't really mind…"

It was extremely difficult for him when she let down her guard like that.

Mahiru was adorable, and when she said those things—words that could make a man lose all control—Amane sighed softly and put his hand on her stomach.

Paying no attention to the way she twisted up as she was being tickled, he slowly traced a path with his fingertip, moving upward from just below her belly button.

He moved his finger at a tantalizing pace, stopping just before the curve of her body changed.

"If I take what you said at face value, it means I can keep going up, you know?"

His fingers weren't mountain climbing yet, but they could easily continue upward and summit those peaks.

In fact, Amane's hands were, as Mahiru had pointed out, rather large and could probably fully envelop those peaks and valleys.

When he made a point of asking if it was all right for him to continue, Mahiru flushed in his arms with such intensity it seemed like she might explode.

She turned her head to look at him with lobster-red cheeks, but Amane didn't mind, and he smiled at her. He didn't stop at just a smile, either, and planted a kiss on her cheek.

"Fooling around includes stuff like this, too."

"…Uh, ah, Amane…"

"Before, I said I didn't really know what fooling around meant. But that was because I didn't include touching you like this…"

Naturally, he hadn't been sure that this kind of touching was all right for a new couple that had only been dating for about two months, so he had been holding back. His intention was to respect Mahiru's wishes.

But since Mahiru had said such provocative things without thinking, he had to speak up and warn her.

"Like I said before, you've got to be careful. I'm a man, after all. I'll really touch you."

"Hmm… B-but your face is red, too, Amane. Can you really do it?"

"That's beside the point."

He was perfectly aware what his own face must look like. And that what he was saying was embarrassing. But it didn't seem like she would get the point if he didn't put it into words, so he had no other choice.

Once Amane had spoken, Mahiru was quiet for a moment, then slowly slipped out of his grasp.

He took her movement as a rejection, but as a bitter smile was rising to his face, Mahiru turned her whole body around and threw her arms around him.

She squeezed him tight, making him intensely aware of her soft skin and sweet scent.

"…Amane, if you really want to touch me…I'll feel embarrassed, but I'll let you," Mahiru mumbled quietly, her voice fragile as she looked up at him.

Amane froze. That was all he could do.

His mind went blank with panic at her expression as she spoke those courageous and lovely words to him.

Mahiru was looking at Amane with trust, though it was mixed with shame and anxiety and just a touch of hope. She seemed ready to accept anything, so long as Amane was the one doing it.

Her expression and demeanor were telling him how much she liked him.

If he were to push her down right then and there, she would be embarrassed, but she would likely still welcome the gesture. The look on her face, her attitude, and her voice were all declaring just how much she trusted and loved him.

She leaned her weight against him as if she was entrusting everything to him. A beat later, Amane's mind started moving again, and his body followed.

The very first thing he did was kiss Mahiru.

She made a little noise in her throat, which sounded unbelievably close.

As he enjoyed the sensation of her lips, softer and dewier than his own, he embraced her delicate body closely and felt it press against his.

Without using his full palm, he simply traced the softness of her curves a little, then gently removed his hand.

After watching Mahiru silently open and close her mouth, her cheeks flushed red, he buried his face in the nape of her neck.

"…The rest can come later."

He added that he didn't think he could stop himself otherwise, and so he started planting kisses on Mahiru's pale neck.

He knew he couldn't leave marks behind, so he limited himself to simple kisses and resolved not to surface until he could stifle the desperate desires bubbling up inside himself.

"Oh my, Mahiru dear, your face is bright red, what's the matter?"

"N-nothing at all…"

Although they had different occupations and workplaces, Amane's parents returned home from their jobs at the same time, and they both seemed puzzled when they looked at Mahiru.

She was sitting on the living room couch, blushing. This was probably because Amane had been kissing her and squeezing her hand at random times all day.

He certainly hadn't attacked her, but perhaps the attention had been a little too much for Mahiru. She seemed embarrassed but happy, however, so Amane preferred to believe that she was pleased about it.

"Amane, don't tell me—," his mother started.

"I swear, I didn't lay a hand on her."

All they had done was a little hugging and light touching. Mahiru was just inexperienced, so she'd felt slightly overwhelmed.

Amane was the same, but he had been faster to recover, and by now he'd regained his composure.

"Not a hand, huh? So just canoodling, then?"

"We kept it wholesome. That's not a problem, is it?"

"You're acting awfully defiant."

"Stop nagging."

"You're always so stingy, Amane. I want to spend some quality time with Mahiru, too."

"Mahiru's mine, so no."

"Well, well."

If he handed Mahiru over to his mother for one moment, she'd hog her for as long as possible, and Amane would definitely regret it. And though Mahiru would enjoy it in her own way, she would likely get worn out, too. He couldn't let his mother monopolize his girlfriend like that.

Mahiru seemed to ruminate a little on the word *mine* and then blushed again. Her reaction caused Amane's mother to grin even harder as she gazed at her son's girlfriend, whose normally pale cheeks were completely flushed. Amane ignored his mother's meaningful smile.

His father, who had been listening in, also broke into a smile.

"Well then, how about we do something together as a family?" he asked.

"Huh?"

"Didn't Miss Shiina say she wanted to go on an outing all together?"

Mahiru had indeed expressed her wishes for a family outing to Amane's parents, but she must not have expected them to bring it up right then. Her caramel-colored eyes blinked rapidly.

"Amane and Miss Shiina will still be here next weekend, so why don't we do just that?"

"Great idea! They came all the way here, and she wants to! ...You're not opposed, right, dear?"

"N-not at all!" Mahiru replied.

"Then, it's decided! Hee-hee, where should we go?"

Mahiru shrank back in awe at Amane's mother, who was

harmoniously discussing with his father where they should go, her voice full of excitement.

Amane was afraid that even if Mahiru herself had asked for this, she might be feeling bad about potentially inconveniencing his parents.

...Both Mom and Dad like Mahiru, of course. That's why they're suggesting an outing...

Even if Amane had been the one to suggest it, he didn't think his parents would have agreed to spend time with someone they didn't personally like.

Just the fact that they were letting her stay over meant they were genuinely fond of her. And they had even brought up going out themselves, so there was no need to worry.

"Prepare yourself," he warned Mahiru. "They're going to drag you all over the place."

"No, I'm really happy and grateful. I don't really have experience with family outings like this..."

Perhaps recalling her childhood, Mahiru put on a strained smile and cast her eyes downward. He could detect a hint of loneliness in the gesture.

Still wearing her same cheerful smile, Amane's mother took a seat beside Mahiru on the sofa, across from Amane.

Without pausing, she embraced Mahiru and patted her head.

"Mahiru, sweetie, you're already part of our family, so you can lean on us as much as you like, okay?" she said.

"In fact, I think they like you even more than their own son," Amane remarked.

"Oh no, are you jealous?" asked his mother.

"No way. I don't mind, since Mahiru's happy."

Mahiru's feelings from a moment earlier seemed to have faded, and now she just looked embarrassed as Amane's mother squeezed her tightly.

That reaction was proof that she was happy, even if she wasn't being up-front about it.

Mahiru was pleased, and as someone who hoped to convince her to take the Fujimiya name someday, Amane welcomed the fact that his parents had taken a liking to her.

He did have mixed feelings about how touchy-feely his mother could be, though.

"My little boy is all grown up," she said.

"Are you making fun of me?"

"No, not at all! I'm just glad I raised a man who cares about the happiness of the person he loves."

"Why are you proud of something so natural...?"

"Hee-hee, men like that are actually quite rare, you know! But it's just what I expect of our child."

"Yeah, yeah."

Surely there was no one on earth who didn't want the people they cared about to be happy. A carefree smile suited Mahiru best.

If she wished it, he wanted to be the one who did the work to make her happy.

Gazing at Mahiru, who was shrinking with embarrassment at his mother's affection, Amane's mouth quietly relaxed into a smile.

Chapter 2

Getting Drenched Was Worth It

"Amane, where are you going?"

Mahiru noticed that Amane was preparing to go out when he stepped into his shoes in the entryway, and she called to him.

She must have been asking because it was fairly late—already past three o'clock in the afternoon.

"Hmm? Oh, I'm stopping by the neighborhood grocery store. Mom asked me to do a little shopping."

This hadn't been Amane's idea.

He'd gotten a message on his phone a moment earlier. Both of his parents were going to be late getting home that evening, so they wouldn't have time to go shopping. They had asked Amane to pick up what they needed instead.

He wasn't doing anything, so he didn't particularly mind, but he wished they had said something in the morning.

"I see," said Mahiru, sounding satisfied with Amane's explanation. Then she knelt down next to him as he sat tying the laces on his sneakers.

His hair must have been a mess. He could feel Mahiru diligently combing through it with her fingers, tidying it up for him. He could also see her at work in the mirror on the wall of the entryway.

"If you're going shopping, do you want me to come with you?"

"Nah, I won't have much to carry, and I'm going to hurry a bit since it looks stormy out. It's no big deal; I'll be fine on my own."

Weather-wise, it seemed likely to rain on them if they took their time. Plus, Amane didn't want to drag Mahiru around on errands when it was so hot, no matter how well the clouds tempered the sun's rays.

He had turned her down with the idea that it would be faster to go alone, since he would return as soon as he finished the shopping.

But when Mahiru answered, she seemed discouraged. "...All right then."

Amane looked up at her in a panic. "Ah, wait, it's not like I don't want you to come or anything!"

"I—I know that. I just kind of wanted to go out together; that's all."

"...We'll go on a date some other time, okay?"

If it was an outing she was after, there would definitely be another opportunity. Plus, girls always seemed to require elaborate preparations to leave the house, so Amane didn't think she'd be ready right that second.

When he gently extended a hand and ruffled her hair, Mahiru opened her eyes a little wider, then put on a fleeting smile and nodded.

"Well then, I'll be waiting for you here," she said.

"Okay."

Amane gave her a small nod, too, then picked up his bag and went out the door.

In the end, it's a good thing I didn't take Mahiru with me, Amane thought keenly.

"…Ugh, sure enough, I got caught in the rain."

He'd thought the clouds had looked menacing, but they were even darker and heavier on his way home. Just as he'd expected, raindrops began falling one after the other out of the sky, soaking his clothes.

Annoyed by the damp fabric sticking to his body, Amane pinched it between his fingers and gently forced some air in between.

Fortunately, everything he had purchased was wrapped in plastic, so it was no problem if it got wet. Amane was the only casualty. By the time he arrived home, he was soaked to the skin.

His bangs clung to his forehead, threatening to obscure his field of vision. After pushing them gently out of the way, he stepped into the entryway, water drip-dropping off his clothes onto the floor. With regret, he realized he should have wrung them out before going inside, but it was too late now.

"Welcome home, Amane. It really poured, didn't it?"

Just as he let out a sigh, he heard the sound of slippers slapping, and Mahiru trotted over to the front door. When she looked at Amane, her eyes went wide.

Mahiru was not expecting him to be so thoroughly soaked. She was holding a small towel, but now it seemed rather useless, considering how drenched he was.

Amane hadn't expected the rain to be so intense, either.

"I'm back. I figured it would just be a passing shower, but it was heavier than I expected."

"If only the weather could have held out until you got home… You'd better warm up in the bath. I've already got it ready."

"Mm, thanks."

He felt a surge of heat in his chest when Mahiru casually took the supermarket bags from his hands, trading them for the little towel with a smile.

He wasn't sure whether he was feeling comforted or blessed. Having such a normal exchange made her seem like part of his family. It gave him a ticklish feeling.

"…This is kind of nice."

"Huh?"

"It's kind of nice to have you get the bath ready and come out to greet me like this."

Amane's parents both worked, so he had rarely seen them in a similar situation. But scenes like this came up often in comics and TV shows, and he had always secretly been jealous of the characters.

Even though it wasn't quite the real thing, this taste of domestic tranquility sent a wonderfully ticklish warmth like spring sunshine through Amane's chest.

He felt indescribable happiness, especially because this scene was playing out with the person he wanted to cherish for the rest of his life.

He smiled slightly at Mahiru. Her cheeks were flushed a faint red, and she was already shrinking back and curling up on herself.

"Well then, I'll go take a bath. Thanks," he said, then slipped past her.

He might have been acting a little out of character, but he couldn't help the smile spreading across his face.

When Amane got out of the bath, Mahiru was sitting quietly on the living room sofa waiting for him. She had a hair dryer at the ready.

There was a dryer by the sink in the bathroom, but she seemed to have anticipated that Amane would fail to use it and had prepared accordingly.

He felt both embarrassed that she had seen right through him and gratified that she understood him so well.

Shaking off his embarrassment in the pleasant chill of the air-conditioned room, he softly approached Mahiru.

"Feeling the AC right out of the bath is great," he said.

"It's nice and cool, but you might catch a cold if you chill yourself too much… Go on, sit there."

"You really don't have to."

"If your hair stays wet, not only can you get chilled and catch a cold, but it's bad for your hair, too."

She told him to quit complaining and sit down, so he obediently took a seat by Mahiru's side. Then she stood up and went around the sofa to plug in the dryer.

She stood behind him getting the water out of his hair with a towel, which also felt sort of ticklish. Not physically so much as emotionally.

"I don't suppose you'll ever get over these sloppy habits of yours, will you, Amane? Sometimes you even come out of the bath with no shirt on."

"Only when it's hot… I'm always fully dressed in winter."

"Because it's cold; I know. But even when it's hot, you can catch a chill if you don't wear a shirt after a hot bath, which can lead to a cold. I won't allow it, not so long as my eyes are black, as they say."

Amane stopped himself from pointing out that Mahiru's eyes were in fact caramel-colored—and that her words implied she intended to stay by his side forever. He just answered obediently that he would be careful and went along with what she wanted.

No matter what she compelled him to agree to, it was pleasant having her look after him.

He felt a little guilty, but having Mahiru dry him off like this felt great.

Once she had carefully absorbed most of the water with the

towel, she used the hair dryer that she had wisely prepared to blow hot air on Amane's hair.

Mahiru obviously took great care of her own hair on a daily basis, and the practiced movements of her hands felt wonderful.

Amane generally didn't like having his hair touched, so this was the first time he had ever thought it felt nice to get his hair blow-dried.

He already liked it when Mahiru touched his hair, so perhaps it was simply a matter of who was doing the touching.

"It's not fair that your hair is this silky even though you don't seem to do anything to take care of it, Amane."

He heard her quietly muttering, almost inaudible under the noise of the hair dryer.

"Oh really? Well, I may not be as meticulous about my grooming as you are, Mahiru, but I'd say I do an ordinary amount."

"You must have good-quality hair to begin with. Your mom and dad both have lovely hair, after all."

"They both pay more attention to their appearance than I do, though. So do you, Mahiru, and for your troubles, you have amazingly smooth and glossy hair."

Mahiru's hair was as shiny as silk, and it felt wonderful to run his fingers through it. Amane could tell how much time and effort she spent caring for it.

He knew this because he played with Mahiru's hair often. It was straight, soft, and fine, and extremely pleasant to the touch. He knew it was easy for fine hair to tangle, but since she groomed it and looked after it, it was never knotted or twisted. It simply drew a lovely straight line down her back. He thought she must be the envy of anyone with unruly hair.

Her straight locks, with their perfect sheen and no split ends, her crowning angel's halo, was so beautiful that anyone would have been

©Hanekoto

jealous. Amane was particularly impressed that she was able to maintain her hair's luster despite its length.

"It's long, though, so it does take a lot of time to look after," she said.

"Well, I guess that only makes sense."

"Of course, I can do or think about other things while I'm tending to it, but it's true that it's a lot of trouble. I've even thought about cutting it off… Amane, which do you prefer, long or short hair?"

"I don't think I really have a preference… Either one would look cute. I like to see you dressed up and enjoying yourself, so I'm happy for you to have it whatever length you like."

Girls didn't always tailor their appearances to appeal to boys, after all. There were plenty of girls who kept their hair long just because they liked it that way.

If Mahiru changed her hairstyle because of some comment from Amane, he would be pleased that she was trying to match his preferences, but he'd also feel bad. It wouldn't make him happy if a stray remark of his caused Mahiru to give up on a style that she had worked so hard to maintain.

He didn't want his words to keep her from doing what she wanted.

"…You think?" she said.

"What about you, Mahiru? Any thoughts about what kind of hairstyle I should have?"

"I would like anything you chose."

"Thought so. I feel the same way."

"…Okay."

Amane didn't turn around, but from Mahiru's voice, he could tell she was smiling bashfully behind him.

It seemed like his answer had been the correct one.

Mahiru was happily working away, until suddenly, the fingers that had been combing through his hair stopped moving.

"…I'd like you with any hairstyle, but—"

"Hmm?"

"When you push your wet hair back with your fingers, it's very…"

"Very…?"

"…Sexy. I mean… It looks cool, I think."

She wasn't telling him what she wanted so much as simply letting her feelings show. But Amane's lips curled into a little smile at Mahiru's admission.

"Should I do it now?" he suggested jokingly.

"N-no, don't! I'll die!" He could tell she was shaking her head vigorously due to the vibrations traveling through her hand.

He was certain that Mahiru must be blushing.

When he tried to turn to see her expression, she used her hand to stop him. It was clear she didn't want to be seen.

…Mahiru's pretty sensitive, huh?

In particular, she was extremely weak to any behavior that reminded her that he was a member of the opposite sex. Amane didn't really go out of his way to point it out or anything, but like the inexperienced girl she was, Mahiru shrank with embarrassment at the slightest hint.

"…I don't think I've really got much sex appeal, though," Amane said.

"Want me to bring you a mirror?" Mahiru replied.

"I just saw myself in the mirror over the sink."

"You must be blind, then."

"Are you sure you're not just seeing me through rose-colored glasses because you like me?"

"I—I won't say that there's absolutely none of that going on, but,

Amane…" The hot air from the dryer stopped. "Listen, when you get out of the bath like this, you let down your defenses, and it just kind of seeps out. You've really got to be more careful," she muttered quietly.

Amane inconspicuously put on a wry smile. Perhaps saying *Love is blind* was going too far, but he had a feeling that he looked particularly good to her precisely because she loved him. But the very fact that Mahiru thought of him that way made him happy.

She would turn as red as a lobster if he teased her too much, so he gave up on questioning her further and settled for shrugging. "Well, I'm not one to talk. If you came and gave me a sultry look after getting out of the bath, I think my knees would go weak."

"I'm pretty sure you've seen me after my bath every day we've been here."

"I've been trying my best not to look directly at you, though."

Since they were staying together in his parents' house, they had been taking their baths one after the other, and they had seen each other afterward wearing their nightclothes.

However, Amane was afraid that if he looked directly at her, he might react in a way the pure and innocent Mahiru wouldn't approve of, so he had been endeavoring not to linger too long in those situations.

Whether he wanted them to or not, though, his desires sometimes reared their ugly heads. Thanks to his efforts to keep them under wraps, Mahiru didn't seem to have noticed, but sometimes he couldn't help himself when she got too assertive.

"I see," Mahiru said. "You've given me some good information."

"Hey, wait a second, why does it sound like you're cooking up a scheme?"

"…Because it's not fair for me to be the only one going around with my heart pounding."

Mahiru didn't seem to realize that the results of getting his heart pounding might not be so good for her heart, either.

That naïveté of Mahiru's was both charming and dangerous. She was too trusting of Amane's courteous and rational nature.

"…You can go ahead and do whatever you want, but I might shut myself away in my room."

"That's not fair." She pouted.

"It's perfectly fair," he replied.

"It is not… I want to be able to push your buttons, Amane."

"No way. You already do enough, without even meaning to. If you're aware of the effect you're having, please be good and try to hold back."

He turned around and cautioned her, but Mahiru didn't seem to accept what he was saying.

He didn't think she'd actually do anything crazy, but she was letting down her guard because they were boyfriend and girlfriend, and that meant Amane had to be careful. It was important for him not to leave any openings that she could exploit.

He turned his gaze directly on Mahiru, who was looking at him somewhat scornfully.

Her glossy caramel eyes met his, and they quickly began to waver, as if they would soon overflow with tears.

Her white porcelain cheeks flushed red, but he paid it no mind and kept staring at her.

Eventually Mahiru was the one who averted her eyes, apparently unable to stand it any longer.

"…Y-you know I can't handle it when you stare at me, Amane."

"Yeah, I know… So are you gonna be good?"

With those last words, he brought his face close to hers and whispered softly, almost sighing. At that, Mahiru let out an utterly adorable shriek and took one step backward.

The hair dryer nearly fell out of her hand, so he casually took it from her. Mahiru looked at him with quivering lips and an expression that said she couldn't believe what he'd done.

Considering her intentions, he probably should have scowled, but that wouldn't have had any impact, so he had stared at her instead.

"…Y-you think that if you use that voice, I'm going to listen to what you say, don't you?" she said.

"I do, and I know you understand that I'm being serious when I speak to you like this. Right?"

"Uh. Th-that's true, but—"

"Anyway, don't try anything funny."

He stared at Mahiru, unwilling to budge. He was being serious, not trying to tease or upset her.

Mahiru seemed to understand that Amane wasn't going to permit any misbehavior, and so she answered, "…All right."

But then, just as Amane was starting to feel relieved, like he could relax his self-control a little, Mahiru came out and said something disquieting. "I've got to find your weak spots, too, Amane."

Since Mahiru had said it out loud, there was no way Amane could pretend he hadn't heard her comment.

"…Next time I have to warn you, I'm gonna whisper it right in your ear," he said.

"F-fine, I'll be careful, I'll be careful!"

Mahiru held her hands over both ears and readied herself to run away.

"Geez." Amane sighed. He'd done something out of character yet again, and he bit his lip hard to try to overcome the following wave of embarrassment.

Chapter 3

An Ideal Look

"Mahiru dear, what about something like this?"

"Ah... It's great! This lace trim is a nice touch, isn't it?"

From one corner of the shop, Amane leisurely watched the two girls—or rather, one woman and one girl—as they shared a pleasant conversation.

Beside him, his father was watching them with the same relaxed gaze.

"Looks like they're both enjoying themselves," his father said.

"Sure does," Amane replied. "...I wonder why women get so excited about clothes?"

On Mahiru's request, the four of them had all gone to the shopping mall together. But as soon as the two ladies began hemming and hawing and holding up clothes to themselves in a boutique, Amane had gotten bored.

It was no real hardship for him to go along on shopping trips or help pick out clothes, but once the chatting and giggling started, the mood became a little too feminine for him to participate, so he kept his distance.

When it came to clothes, Amane never spent much time making

decisions. So as he watched Mahiru and his mother having a pleasant chat while trying to choose the best outfit, he fell into a strange mood.

Amane's father was standing with him, watching the two excited ladies. Usually, he would have joined in with them, but it seemed he was hanging back to keep Amane company.

"Maybe it's because, no matter how much time passes, girls still want to be the most beautiful versions of themselves. Also, they seem to simply enjoy getting dressed up."

"Well, it's fun to watch anyway."

"You mean to see them dressed up?"

"That too, but I meant watching them have so much fun choosing."

A lot of guys seemed to find it annoying when they had to accompany girls on shopping trips. But Amane had been forced to go along with his mother on plenty of such outings, so he was used to it. Plus, he wasn't an impatient person and could always find a way to entertain himself.

Besides, when it came to Mahiru, Amane was perfectly satisfied just to see her smiling happily. That was all it took for him to be satisfied.

"Oh, so you've finally started appreciating it, huh, Amane? That's good."

"I don't know about appreciating it or whatever, but I think anyone would have fun watching the person they love enjoying themselves."

"I think that's a great feeling to have. Even being bored doesn't mean you're a bad guy, but if your irritation shows on your face, it ruins the atmosphere. On the other hand, if you're able to find the fun in it, you don't need to worry about all that, and you can have a good time together, right?"

"…Yeah, I'm glad I don't have any issues with that."

Amane was the kind of person who preferred to take it easy until pressed by some necessity—and who could pass the time doing nothing at all. So he was content to take it easy and observe the two women like this. His nature allowed him to find happiness in such moments, which was a rare quality.

"…Watching Mahiru getting along with Mom so well, like they're really mother and daughter, makes me glad we came."

Being left to himself felt just a little bit lonely, but even more than that, he was relieved.

Even if it wasn't exactly the real thing, Mahiru must have wished for this sort of family scene without ever expecting it to happen. And now it was finally happening. It filled Amane with an irrepressible happiness.

Mahiru was smiling without a care, not as some perfect angel, but as an ordinary girl her age. It was such a calm and happy scene that Amane's heart felt full just watching from the sidelines.

"So any plans to actually make them mother and daughter?" his father asked.

"Is that something I have to tell you right now, Dad?"

"Oops, sorry, that was rude of me. I'm not the one who should be asking." His father put on an easy smile and didn't question Amane any further.

Having a father who was so quick to understand these things could be complicated in its own way, but for the moment, Amane was happy to be worried about something so trivial.

It was much better than being interrogated by his mother anyway. So as long as his father wasn't going to press the issue further, Amane was content.

"Shuuto, Amane, what are you doing all the way over there? Come here."

Apparently his mother had noticed the two of them calmly standing by, and she beckoned them over.

Mahiru was looking their way, too.

She was holding two articles of clothing.

Since they had been summoned, father and son walked over together. With a cheery grin, Amane's mother stood behind Mahiru, hands on her shoulders, and gently pushed the girl forward so she stood before Amane.

"Amane, between these two tops, which do you think suits Mahiru better?"

She seemed to want him to choose a piece of clothing.

Amane glanced at what she was holding and saw one fancy, feminine blouse trimmed with lace at the sleeves and hem and one pastel-blue blouse that was more subdued but had a cheerful look.

He honestly thought that either one of them would suit her. And since Mahiru would be the one buying it, he figured it was probably best not to give too much direction.

"I think whichever one Mahiru likes best will be just fine."

"…W-well, I'd like to hear your opinion, too, Amane. I want to know what kinds of things you like…"

Mahiru cast her eyes down bashfully for a moment, then looked back up at him in timid expectation. Amane gulped.

Simply knowing that she cared about what he thought had his heart pounding violently.

It was true that he liked Mahiru just as she was, but he was overjoyed at the idea that she would dress herself in clothes he liked, just for him.

Fully aware that his cheeks were turning red, Amane looked back and forth between the blouses and Mahiru's face, then pointed to the one trimmed in lace.

"This one."

©Hanekoto

Mahiru smiled and held the shirt that Amane had chosen a little closer, then went to go return the other one.

"…She's really adorable, isn't she?" Amane's mother remarked.

"Don't I know it," he replied.

"It seems like she's starting to come out of her shell."

"Oh, be quiet."

When he heard the amusement in his mother's voice, Amane sulkily turned away.

After Mahiru bought her clothes and they left the shop, Amane and his family wandered aimlessly around the mall.

Just walking through the complex, supposedly the largest in the whole prefecture, was surprisingly enjoyable. However, they attracted a lot of looks, which sparked complicated feelings in Amane.

His parents were objectively good-looking, as was Mahiru, and a group of attractive people was certain to draw attention.

Mahiru was no stranger to such attention, so she didn't seem to mind it at all. She was snuggled up against Amane's arm.

However, though she was used to turning heads, it seemed she felt embarrassed walking along with her arm wrapped around Amane's because her cheeks were faintly flushed.

For his part, it was almost impossible to keep calm with Mahiru's softness pressed against him. But he was sure that his mother would tease him if he showed any signs of distress, so he awkwardly maintained his best poker face.

Amane gripped the bag containing the clothes Mahiru had purchased and tried to turn his mind away from the feeling. But when he did that, Mahiru clung even tighter, as if questioning why he wasn't looking at her, which made ignoring the sensation extremely difficult.

"Mahiru, um, so—"

"Yes?"

"...Ah, well, um."

"What is it?"

"...Come to think of it, you haven't worn the outfit that you bought over Golden Week, have you?"

He was conflicted over whether to point out that her chest was touching him, but every so often, Mahiru would impishly press against him on purpose, so after puzzling over what he should do, he decided to bring up a completely different subject.

Mahiru's outfit that day was a tidy little dress with a breezy, elegant design, not the off-the-shoulder one she had previously purchased.

She'd said she was going to wear the latter for him, but in the end, he had never seen it, so he wondered what had happened.

Mahiru blinked her eyes at the mention of Golden Week, then looked a little sheepish.

"...I decided I wanted to wear it when the two of us go on a date."

"...O-oh, you did?"

"You'll take me out, won't you?" Mahiru was irresistibly adorable as she softly nestled up to him, their arms intertwined.

Amane gently squeezed her hand. "...Sure, all right. Why don't we go somewhere together? This is a family outing, after all. That's different from a date."

"...R-right."

"Where do you want to go?"

"As long as I'm with you, Amane, anywhere is fine."

"When you say something like that, it makes me not want to go out at all. I'd be happy to have you dress up, but I don't want to show you to other people."

"...It sounds like you want to have a date at home. Well, that's fine with me. It looks like we won't have good weather for the next few days anyway."

Now that she mentioned it, Amane remembered seeing on the

weekend forecast that things weren't looking promising. A typhoon was gradually approaching.

It wasn't going to hit them directly, but they would see the effects, and it was likely to rain.

Amane had figured that the typhoon might blow past while he was visiting, but since it was his long-awaited homecoming, he had hoped they would have good weather anyway.

Considering the situation, they might not be able to go anywhere. But Mahiru seemed to place more importance on spending time with him and didn't seem too hung up on actually going out.

Amane made up his mind to check the weather when they got home, and he squeezed Mahiru's hand again.

"I guess I'm also happy with whatever, so long as I'm with you, Mahiru. How about we check the weather later and pick a day?"

"Okay."

"...I thought you two were just back there flirting, but you were making plans for a date, weren't you?" his mother interjected in a mischievous voice.

"Sorry to disappoint you," Amane said, calmly shutting her down, "but we were already set on it."

Walking in front of them, Amane's parents shared a little smile.

But rather than teasing, they seemed to be pleased. They turned around without questioning the teenagers further, and Amane snorted quietly and tugged on Mahiru's hand.

Chapter 4

A Stay-at-Home Date with the Angel

The worries they'd had while shopping had proved warranted. It wasn't just drizzling, it was pouring. Sheets of water noisily pelted the ground. Amane and Mahiru looked at each other and nodded seriously.

"Rain, huh?"

"Yes, rain."

They had expected as much when they'd heard the weather forecast, but a long spell of rain had started the very day they'd planned to go out and still hadn't let up, and now they weren't sure what to do.

Thankfully, the wind wasn't that strong, and it wasn't going to rain hard enough for a state of emergency to be declared, so Amane's parents had already left for work.

His parents couldn't stay home from work, but Amane and Mahiru's outing wasn't essential.

There wasn't anything truly stopping them from going out, but in weather like this, their clothes would likely get ruined, and if they got drenched and caught colds, it would be no laughing matter.

"I don't think we should," Amane said. "I'm not ready to get soaked to the bone."

"We could both end up catching colds, so let's scrap the idea," Mahiru agreed.

"Okay. Well, I guess we can just relax at home."

Both of them preferred the indoors anyway, so it was no problem staying at home. It was unfortunate that they'd lost the chance to go out on their date, but the alternative wasn't so terrible, either.

Amane quickly abandoned their plans, chalking it up to bad timing. But Mahiru's shoulders were drooping in disappointment.

Amane ruffled her hair. "Don't look so bummed. We can go out again another time, right?"

"I know. It's just too bad that this had to happen when we went to all the trouble of making plans."

"You wanted to go on a date that badly?"

"Of course I did."

"R-right, I see... I'm sorry to cancel when you were looking forward to it so much."

In the face of her frank admission, Amane felt awkward, and his cheeks tightened up strangely. Thankfully, Mahiru was looking out the window, so she didn't seem to notice the change that came over him.

"Putting that aside, I'm happy to spend some time relaxing with you, Amane... Though I could do without you constantly touching my ears like you did the other day."

"What, are you trying to remind me so I'll touch them again?"

"Not a chance! If you keep touching and whispering in my ears, you'll drive me to an early grave!"

"An early grave, huh? I think the real problem is how sensitive you are to me."

"You're exactly the same, though."

He couldn't argue with that. However, Amane was sure he would never react to anything with as much sensitivity as Mahiru.

If he touched one of her sensitive spots, that alone was enough to make her tremble and curl up in a ball, so it was hard to know how aggressive he could be. She was the type of girl who might run away or go pout if he overdid it and overwhelmed her, so it was difficult to judge the right degree of contact.

"I don't have as many weak spots as you do, Mahiru, so I'm not going to bend that easily."

"I—I told you, didn't I? I'm going to make you cave."

"…You're already caving, and we haven't even done anything."

He smiled at how carelessly Mahiru had revealed the sensitivity of her ears. Her red face made it clear she regretted the admission.

From the way she behaved, it had long been obvious that every time he touched her ears or whispered into one of them, her knees gave out dramatically, so it was a little late to be pointing it out now. But it seemed Mahiru hadn't wanted him to find out.

"…Now that it's come to this, I'll have to use every possible means to get you to fall madly in love with me, Amane."

"What could you possibly do, when I'm already crazy about you…?"

Leaving aside the question of caving, Amane was already captivated by Mahiru. He only had eyes for her. It would be difficult to make him fall any harder.

If he loved Mahiru any more ardently than he already did, he would lose all self-control and would have to shut himself away.

"…You say things like that so smoothly, Amane."

"Well, it *does* embarrass me. But I've often heard that things turn sour if you can't communicate with words. We're dating, so there shouldn't be a problem with me telling you how I feel. And we're human, so we ought to be able to find some mutual understanding by talking things over."

Amane had the feeling that he had said something similar once before. Even if they were both in love with one another, sometimes it wasn't enough just to show it with their behavior. By communicating openly before things turned sour, they could both avoid extra dissatisfaction and stress.

If a word could erase even the smallest seed of discontent, then it was worth the effort. In fact, Amane didn't even think of it as effort.

He used his words so they wouldn't talk past one another, yes. But the number one reason why he spoke so frankly was that Mahiru's reactions were always extremely adorable, and he enjoyed watching her—though, he couldn't tell her that.

"...I love how logical you are, too."

"Mm, thanks... I've noticed that since we started dating, you've been saying you love me a lot."

"Th-that's, um, well the word just comes gushing out, and I can't help saying it."

"...Oh."

From the way Mahiru was mumbling with embarrassment, it was plain to see that her comment was not meant as shallow flattery.

From the beginning, Mahiru had never been anything less than genuine with Amane. Even before they were dating, whenever she criticized him harshly, she was speaking her true opinion. These days, she was probably biased by her affection, but she never said anything she didn't truly believe, so her words just now must also have been from the heart.

It was extremely embarrassing to be caught off guard like this, with her saying such things straight to his face. Without meaning to, he let his eyes wander around the room. Mahiru seemed to take notice.

"I embarrassed you just now, didn't I?"

"Is that so bad?"

"No. I just feel like I finally scored a point today."

"…Finally? But the day's just started."

"In that case, I might get quite a lead on you, Amane."

"I don't think there's any chance of that."

"What do you mean?"

"Just making a prediction based on what usually happens."

"…It sounds like you want me to blow your mind."

"Do your worst."

To tell the truth, he wanted her to keep things at a moderate level, but it was clear that this was an expression of Mahiru's love for him, and so he didn't want to dismiss it.

When he looked at her as if to say *Give it your best shot,* for some reason a confident smile spread across her face, and she pulled a plastic case out of a cardboard box sitting on the table.

"Then allow me to start with this," she said.

"Wait a sec; where did you get that?"

Amane immediately recognized the thing Mahiru had pulled out. Inside the plastic case was a disc labeled in bold permanent marker: GROWING UP—ONE YEAR OLD.

As soon as he saw it, he wanted to quip that it was not the kind of mind-blowing that he was expecting.

"From your mother's collection, of course."

"…Why did she give it to you?"

"She said that if it turned out we had to stay in, we could watch this instead. She laid out all sorts of drama DVDs, too."

Amane's parents were the types to watch any genre of movie, Western or Japanese, and they kept a fair collection of DVDs at home. While that would certainly suffice for killing time, Amane couldn't believe that his mother would slip in a home video when she handed them over to Mahiru.

Come to think of it, she showed Mahiru that photo album without my permission, so maybe it's not that far-fetched.

In fact, whether he believed it or not, his mother had already handed over the video, so all he could do now was curse his bad luck.

"...So am I right that you don't really like looking back on things like this?"

"It's not that I hate it, but it's hard to sit down and enjoy a video full of my own past embarrassments."

Mahiru had seen the photo album, so in a way it was already too late, but there was a world of difference between photos and video.

Amane didn't think his parents had kept anything truly humiliating, but this was his mother's doing, and he wasn't sure how far he could trust her.

Amane wasn't too thrilled about watching the DVD, but if Mahiru wanted to, he would allow it, though he would have liked to inspect it first.

"Did you really do anything you'd need to be ashamed of?" she asked.

"I was a much naughtier kid than you think, Mahiru..."

"My indoors-y Amane?"

"I feel like you're implying something there... But anyway, I was just a normal kid; that's all."

Although the photographs didn't really make it obvious, Amane had been an extremely active boy when he was little. He had gone out exploring with other children his age and played at the houses of kids of all ages. He'd been bursting with a friendliness and energy hard to imagine now.

Looking back on it, Amane thought that he had probably grown up a healthy little rascal precisely because the adults in the community had kept a friendly eye out for all the children.

Though, now I've settled down to the point where it's hard to believe I was ever a rascal.

"…Now I want to see it even more. I bet you used to go around greeting everyone in your neighborhood with a big smile, didn't you?"

"…Well, I think I was pretty friendly."

He remembered having an extremely good reputation with people his mother's age and older. Though he had probably gotten a boost from his mother's own popularity.

"I bet you were super cute when you were little, Amane."

"…If you want to watch the video, you can, but I don't think it will be that interesting."

"Don't say that! I'm excited to see a side of you that I don't know."

"…Do whatever you like."

He didn't feel like stopping her, since she was holding up the DVD case in such high spirits. Though Amane was somewhat reluctant, he figured he could probably stand a bit of embarrassment and decided to let Mahiru do as she pleased.

"When I was growing up, no one really took photos or videos of me, so I think it's kind of nice that you have things like this," Mahiru mumbled as she carefully embraced the DVD case.

Amane watched her, pretending he hadn't heard a thing.

He didn't want to make too much of it, since she had said it in a particularly dispirited tone of voice, but when he looked at her expression, he saw that her smile was a little lonesome. It didn't linger, however, but flitted past, like the twinge of an old scar.

Amane pursed his lips automatically when he thought about how Mahiru's parents had neglected her. But he figured it would only make her uncomfortable now to know how angry he was.

That was why he had sworn in his heart to never let her experience such loneliness again.

"…Mahiru, does that mean you're the kind who likes to keep childhood records?"

"It's lonely not to have anything, so I guess I do. I think both good memories and bad can help you grow when you look back at them later with a new perspective."

"Well, in that case, when it comes time for all that, we'll have to take lots of pictures and videos like this—and leave plenty of records."

He swiftly took the DVD case from Mahiru's hands and put the disc into the player.

Although he didn't mention what he'd meant by "all that," Amane had already made up his mind, and his resolution and love were unwavering. He had confidence in his instincts. He was going to give Mahiru the thing she craved from the bottom of her heart—no, they were going to build it together, he was sure of it.

He didn't know how she had taken his words, but when he finished setting up the DVD and returned to Mahiru's side on the sofa, he could see her infinitely genuine eyes were open wide and blinking quickly.

"Something the matter?" he asked.

"N-no, nothing at all…!"

It seemed like she was having difficulty settling on a reaction. Many different emotions flashed in her eyes as Amane watched, smiling. His gaze seemed to be embarrassing her.

After clearing her throat, Mahiru shifted her gaze to the DVD footage that had begun to play back.

This is the kind of thing we'll just have to take slowly.

Amane was still a child, unable to take full responsibility.

Putting his ideals into words was easy, but he lacked just about everything he needed to turn them into reality. Life was not so easy that good intentions alone could ensure everything would turn out all right.

The first thing he had to do was gradually prove to her that the passion behind his feelings was everlasting.

Feeling that warmth settle deep in his chest, he smiled at Mahiru, who was fidgeting a little beside him.

"Well, here's the video of my childhood you were so eager to see. I think anyone's cute when they're that age, though."

"…You were a cute kid," Mahiru mumbled while watching the footage. "I can see traces of it when I look at you now, but as expected, the expression in your eyes was softer back then, huh?" She seemed to have pulled herself together.

With a wry smile, Amane responded, "I guess these days I do look a little mean."

In the past, he'd had quite a childish and androgynous face, and even Amane, who didn't have much self-confidence, thought he was a cute kid.

All sorts of scenes played before them. Some of them Amane didn't really remember, and others he did. They saw Amane chatting and smiling at the neighbors as they strolled by walking their dogs, Amane playing innocently with other children in the park, and young Amane with his delighted mother, riding a bicycle for the first time.

Mahiru was absorbed in the images, and it seemed like their earlier conversation might have temporarily left her mind. As for Amane, he couldn't help but wish that, if possible, she would forget this instead.

"Oh, that boy showed up before, too, right?"

They'd only been watching for about an hour, but several years had passed by in the video.

They had watched many scenes of Amane playing with other children, and it must have caught her eye that, while the other faces changed, one particular boy appeared time after time.

"Ah, that's someone my age who lived in the neighborhood. I guess you could call us childhood friends. We had kind of a complicated relationship, but I was fairly good friends with him."

At this point, it was nostalgic for Amane to look back at a time when they had been close, but he didn't feel any lingering attachment or desire to return to those days.

Amane couldn't say with any confidence that he liked how he was now, but he was working toward becoming a version of himself that he could be proud of without reservation, so he felt no pull to return to a time when he was carefree and naive about the world.

Amane had smoothly deflected Mahiru's question, so without saying anything else, she turned her gaze back to the television.

The youthful, somewhat shrill voice of the boy in the video told him that his childhood self was in high spirits.

As he watched himself covered in dirt from frolicking too much in the summertime, his mind flooded with memories of a different time.

"...Amane, you really were way more of a little rascal than I expected."

"I mean, I was a kid. I did all sorts of things, got scolded by my mother, and learned better... Wait, Mahiru, we can't watch this next part."

When the video moved into the hallway of his house, Amane remembered what had been filmed next. In a panic, he grabbed the remote control and smashed the PAUSE button.

He'd moved so suddenly that Mahiru stiffened in her seat. But for the sake of his dignity and the purity of Mahiru's eyes, he simply couldn't let her see it.

"Huh, why did you pause?" she asked.

"Well, I have a feeling what comes next is kind of inappropriate. It's shameful for me, but more importantly, it'll be embarrassing for you to watch."

"...Are you being honest? Or do you just not want to show it to me?"

"Well, that's part of it, but not all. You won't be able to look me in the eye afterward."

Amane didn't want her to see him in such a state, and he wasn't interested in seeing it, either. And Mahiru being Mahiru, if she saw it, she might be rendered temporarily speechless.

He wasn't sure how to explain the problem to her as she looked at him with suspicion, but he figured she would understand best if he said it directly. He took a deep breath and braced himself.

"…Well, um, I'm sure you know that at the end of this hallway is the bathroom. It's a video of me getting a bath."

He looked at Mahiru as if to ask whether she wanted to see a naked boy, even if he was a child under the age of five, and she stiffened. Apparently, the truth had caught her by surprise.

Amane would have liked to complain to his mother about keeping such unsavory mementos, but she wasn't there to criticize.

"…S-sorry for asking," Mahiru said at last.

"It's fine, so long as you understand. I wish my parents had been more sensitive about what parts of my childhood they decided to film."

"N-no kidding."

Amane figured that they'd seen enough home movies and stopped the tape, but Mahiru put on a slightly regretful expression and deliberately shrugged.

"…Oh, were you interested, after all?" he said teasingly.

"D-don't make me out to be a pervert, please!"

"You just seemed a little curious is al— *Ouch!* Okay, okay. I know you didn't want to see it, so please don't head-butt me."

He'd only been joking, but Mahiru seemed to take it seriously. She smooshed her bright-red face into his shoulder and looked like she was sulking, so he offered her an honest apology.

Mahiru spent a moment grinding her head into his arm. She was giving off a lot of heat. Slowly, she rose to meet Amane's gaze and stuck out her lip in a pout.

"...Amane, you're a bully."

"I said I was sorry. Come on, cheer up, okay?"

She seemed likely to pull away from him if he teased her too much, so he clasped one of her tense hands and gave her the kindest smile he could muster. Mahiru pressed her lips tightly together and looked at him with dissatisfaction.

"...I'm sure you would be curious if you were in my position, Amane."

"I dunno; I don't really have any interest in children... And didn't you basically just admit you were curious?"

"I did not! Stupid!"

By the time he realized he'd gone too far, it was too late. Mahiru slipped out of Amane's gentle hold and slapped at his thighs.

He must have hit the nail on the head, he thought. As indescribably embarrassed and self-conscious as it made him, he still felt happy that she had shown an interest. Fearing that he might smile against his better judgment, he decided to head to the kitchen to fix drinks, hoping that might help Mahiru settle down.

Trying to give her some space to cool off, Amane took a little extra time and prepared one of the sweet drinks Mahiru seemed to like. But when he returned to the living room, she was glaring daggers at him.

"Come on, snap out of it. I brought you some homemade iced cocoa."

"...If you think you can bribe me into a good mood, you're sorely mistaken."

"You don't want it?"

"N-no, I do, but... Good grief."

It seemed like Mahiru was going to accept the offering, after all.

Smiling inconspicuously, so that she wouldn't see, Amane politely handed it over.

This cocoa required a bit of effort to make. You had to dissolve a very strong paste with milk in a pan and then chill the mixture with ice. It was one of Mahiru's favorite drinks.

Because it had to be made in a pan, the cleanup took some effort, too, so Amane rarely made the drink for himself. But when he made it for Mahiru after thoughtlessly hurting her feelings, she would gracefully accept the bribe and listen to what he had to say.

After confirming she had taken a sip, he asked, "Is the flavor all right?"

Her accusatory gaze softened somewhat. "…It's good."

"Glad to hear it."

"Are you sure you're not trying to weasel your way out of this with a tasty treat?"

"…I would never."

Mahiru glanced at Amane, who was smiling wryly, and stood up with the mug of cocoa still in her hand.

Amane broke into a cold sweat, worried that she had been so offended that she was going to go back to the guest room. But Mahiru immediately sat back down, and his worry subsided.

Now he had a different reason to sweat.

"…Mahiru?"

"…The air conditioner is on, so I'm feeling cold."

Mahiru had taken a seat in between Amane's legs. She looked up at him with an impish smile.

Amane let out a very deep sigh that was part relief and part reluctance.

"How far do you want to go?"

"I don't mind letting you do as you please, but if you try to go too far, I think you know what will happen to the cocoa, right?"

©Hanekoto

The other day, she had said she liked being touched, but it was clear that this was payback.

"It will probably spill on you."

"Yes, it sure will."

"In that case, I won't do anything."

"Fine by me."

It was a bold strategy, using herself as a hostage, but it was very effective against Amane.

He hadn't been planning to do anything either way, but since Mahiru was directly and deliberately driving her point home, he smiled as well and spread both arms to emphasize his innocence, striking a pose that made it clear he wasn't doing a thing.

"The draft between us is cold," she said.

"You've gotten a little demanding, haven't you, Mahiru?"

"You don't like me making demands?"

"I never said that. Actually, I wish you would do it more."

Mahiru was usually very self-disciplined, and he hoped she would at least allow her boyfriend to spoil her silly. If she had any wish that Amane could grant, he intended to do it. He was ready to deny himself anything, if it would only make Mahiru smile.

However, Mahiru seemed to feel the same way, and she was always spoiling him, so often a quiet struggle would break out between them over who would take the initiative… But that day, it seemed Mahiru was going to be agreeable and let him spoil her.

Mahiru looked relaxed as she sipped her iced cocoa. She was leaning her whole weight against Amane as he held her

" .Oh, I just noticed you didn't make yourself any, Amane."

"I'm not that fond of sweets. And besides, I feel fulfilled just watching you drink yours."

Simply gazing at Mahiru as she relished the cocoa with a smile was gratifying enough for Amane. He didn't need his own cup.

"We haven't even had lunch yet," she said, "and you're already full."

"I meant spiritually fulfilled."

"So you don't want lunch?"

"I do, I do."

Those are two completely different issues, Amane thought. With his arms wrapped around Mahiru's body, he gently squeezed to emphasize his point. When he did, she chuckled in his arms.

"You're quick to change your mind," she said. "Amane, you're perfectly capable of cooking something by now."

"…I want to eat what you make, Mahiru, and I won't be satisfied by anything else. Though, I feel bad making you do all the work."

Even as he spoke, he was aware that he sounded kind of pathetic. But he had gotten so used to eating Mahiru's cooking that any other food now seemed flavorless.

Of course, that didn't mean he couldn't eat it. He just found it lacking.

"Oh, you're hopeless."

"I know full well that you captured my heart through my stomach, Mahiru."

"Feel free to keep going until you can't live without me."

"I'm already there."

In the time he had spent with Mahiru, Amane had learned to take decent care of himself. But being with her was what made life worth living.

After all, this was the first time he had ever cared so much about and wanted to treasure someone else, so he couldn't help but feel like the world would lose its color if he was torn away from her.

If he had to live on his own again, trudging through those uneventful, colorless days would be akin to a living death.

It wasn't just her cooking. Mahiru's very presence was part of what made Amane who he was now, and so he couldn't live without her. That was the meaning behind his response. But Mahiru's body noticeably stiffened.

"Y-you really have a way of putting things, Amane."

"What way would that be?"

"Never mind. Okay, all right, I'll make lunch."

Mahiru drained the remaining half of her cocoa and stood up. Amane looked at her, a little regretful that her warmth and softness had disappeared from his grasp.

"You don't want to take your time drinking the cocoa?"

"And whose fault do you think it is that I can't...? I—I finished my drink, so I'm going to go cook. It's lunchtime already anyway!"

When Amane followed Mahiru's finger and looked at the clock, he saw that it was indeed past noon.

"Oh, you're right, it *is* lunchtime. Um, I can help, or—"

"Not today!"

It seemed like she was just making up an excuse to escape. But before he was able to point that out, she'd already fled to the kitchen. So Amane pretended like he hadn't heard anything and silently thanked Mahiru for cooking his meal.

After they had eaten lunch, while Amane was washing the dishes, he suddenly realized Mahiru had disappeared.

It wasn't like they always had to be together, but since she had slipped away unnoticed, he couldn't help wondering what had happened. Did she have something to take care of? Or had she suddenly felt unwell?

Thinking back to their earlier exchange, she had seemed completely normal after their meal, so he didn't think she'd disappeared to sulk, but he couldn't completely write off the possibility, either.

He decided to go check on her and turned off the water. But with truly perfect timing, he immediately heard someone coming down the stairs.

The footsteps were lighter than his own, and when he turned around to look in their direction, he froze.

He was glad he hadn't been holding any plates. If he had, they probably would have splashed back into the sink.

"So since we're having our long-awaited stay-at-home date, I thought I would wear the outfit I had prepared for it."

Mahiru had on the off-the-shoulder dress she had mentioned the other day, looking as if she was trying to hide her embarrassment.

She normally didn't wear very revealing outfits—at most, she might put something over a sleeveless top. But now she was showing everything from her neck down to her shoulders, even her collarbone.

All that skin, normally never exposed, was right out in the open, and though the sky outdoors was covered by thick dark-gray clouds, the space around Mahiru seemed bright and dazzling.

The sleeves of the dress were three-quarter length, so they didn't show as much as a sleeveless top would have. But the places it *did* expose were normally covered up, which made a greater impression.

"What do you think, does it suit me?" she asked.

"It does. It looks amazing on you."

In fact, the sight had been so striking that Amane had accidentally forgotten to compliment her. Under Mahiru's pointed gaze, he hurried to react.

Sure, Amane had said he thought the dress would suit her when she bought it, but he had never expected it to be such a knockout.

It didn't show a lot of skin, really, but it had a subtle sensuality that nevertheless meshed with Mahiru's clean image—probably aided by her poise and features.

"…Thank you," she replied.

"Maybe it would be better if I gave you more specific compliments? You've got beautiful skin, so when you show it off like this, you're positively radiant. Plus, outfits that emphasize your slim figure are perfect. This way, the clothes complement your natural beauty, rather than steal away the attention. Also, you look taller than usual in a dress with this sort of design. I think it looks refined and makes you seem more mature."

His vocabulary on the topic was lacking, so he wasn't sure if he was doing a good job complimenting her. But since she had gotten all dressed up for him, he used every word he knew trying to praise her.

Mahiru got flustered and shook her head.

"I—I get it, okay, that's enough! What are you trying to do, make me blush?"

"I'm just saying what I want to say. Watching you blush from the compliments is a bonus."

He wasn't flattering Mahiru; he was truly complimenting her, and doing so satisfied him, so it wasn't like he was trying to get her to do anything in particular.

He felt like his heart would overflow if he didn't put his feelings into words and expel them.

"Thank you very much. But n-no more, I'm quite full."

"Is that because we just ate lunch?"

"I—I feel like you're just getting revenge for earlier…"

"Whatever could you be talking about?"

He was being deliberately cheeky, but the praise he had heaped on her was genuine and true.

However, he was worried that if he overdid it, Mahiru might become too flustered to speak. So he left things there and dried his hands with the towel he had laid out.

"Well then, I'm finished with washing the dishes, and I took care of the housework I was asked to do earlier, so what should we do now?"

Mahiru had gone to the trouble of changing clothes, but the weather had remained the same—it was still raining.

The news had said the typhoon wouldn't move away before late that night, and it seemed that the forecast was right on the money.

There were limits to the things the two of them could do in his parents' house.

They had already looked at home videos earlier. They could watch a film, or read some of the books in the study, or else dutifully get started on their schoolwork.

Those were the things Amane usually did when he was at home, but they seemed too ordinary for a date.

"...I just want to relax and spend time with you, Amane; would that be okay?"

"It's totally fine with me, but won't you get bored?"

"Of course not, I'm the one who suggested it. I'm plenty satisfied just being by your side."

Mahiru was as adorable as ever. Amane felt himself smile as he softly patted her head.

"Okay. Then I guess we can just kick back. Though, since this is my parents' house, there aren't a ton of things we can do to amuse ourselves."

All the games and movies that Amane would usually enjoy with Mahiru were back in his own apartment. He'd left them behind in order to save luggage space, but now he was thinking that he should have brought at least one game.

However, he also knew from experience that the two of them could be perfectly happy even without such things, and that was certainly more economical, he thought wryly.

"Feeling satisfied just by being together saves a lot of energy, doesn't it?" he said.

"Heh-heh, so it does. I bet that's the trick to staying together long-term, you know?"

"I don't think that really counts as a trick. More a matter of compatibility and character, but…there's no question that the two of us mesh well."

With friends and lovers, Amane felt that the key to longevity wasn't whether two people had fun together, but whether they could endure the silent times. For that reason, he figured he and Mahiru, who both felt completely satisfied even when they weren't talking, must be extremely compatible.

Though that day they were on a date, so of course they were talking and paying attention to each other.

"Want to go to my room? …Not for anything inappropriate, just in case you were wondering."

"Of course! I never suspected you meant anything else."

"I kind of wish you would, actually…"

Mahiru seemed prepared to allow him to do just about anything, but he had mixed feelings about not being the subject of even a little suspicion.

Smiling wryly at Mahiru's exceptional degree of confidence in him, Amane led her by the hand to his room.

The majority of the furniture had been taken out, so the space was rather empty. But that only made Mahiru's splendid presence all the more conspicuous.

Amane briefly worried about where they would sit, before climbing onto the bed and taking a seat where the soft surface wouldn't hurt Mahiru's backside. She cast her eyes downward, looking a little embarrassed, but then sat down naturally between Amane's legs and leaned back against him.

He felt joy and hesitation as he noted that her attitude of complete trust really got him going. Despite his feelings, however, Amane kept a firm lid on his urges as he embraced her.

This time, he held her even tighter.

Careful not to hurt her, he pulled Mahiru's body close so he could experience her softness and warmth. When he put his chin on one of her smooth shoulders and leaned against her, Mahiru shuddered slightly.

"...Ah, um, Amane?"

"Surely this is fine, right? I'm not touching anything I shouldn't."

The parts he was touching were her stomach and back, as well as her shoulders.

Since Mahiru had changed clothes, the skin beneath his chin was uncovered, and he could feel its silky texture directly.

When he stealthily glanced down, he saw that her décolletage was exposed by her off-the-shoulder dress, so the luxurious swells and valley of cleavage were peeking out of her clothing.

It was a superb view, but if he looked too long, wicked thoughts would rise to his mind, so Amane pulled away his gaze and planted a kiss on one of her ears, which had turned bright red.

"Hya! ...I—I thought I told you this morning to stop playing with my ears."

"Or you'll go weak in the knees?"

"I-it's not that bad, but...it makes me restless, so you shouldn't do it."

"All right, I'll stop. But only so that I have a trump card later."

Rather than teasing her all the time, it would probably be more effective to touch her ears only on special occasions. If she got used to it, the thrill she felt would grow dull, so it was best not to overdo it. For the time being, he set aside the question of what was best from Mahiru's perspective.

"That sounds just as bad."

"Or I could get you used to it now?"

"I don't like either option!"

Mahiru looked back forcefully, and this time she was glaring intensely at him with a bright-red face.

He could tell that she would start sulking again if he overdid it, so Amane tenderly whispered he was sorry and wrapped his arms around her body again.

"...You tease too much, Amane."

"Sorry, sorry, I won't do it again... At any rate, that dress looks amazing on you. It looks so good it would be a waste to show it to anyone else, so I'm glad we're relaxing at home."

Frankly, most of Mahiru's clothes were very stylish, and this outfit was no exception. The off-the-shoulder dress suited her perfectly. She made it her own, more than any model could have.

With her smooth shoulders and defenseless décolletage so exposed, Amane honestly didn't want anyone else to see her.

He hated the idea of other men looking at her kissable, porcelain skin, in perfect health thanks to her untiring efforts. As he gazed at it, he even found himself a little grateful for the bad weather.

"...I can easily tell that this sort of dress is to your liking, Amane."

"T-to my liking? I just think it looks good on you. Simple clothes with some accents suit you. More than flashy outfits, at least."

"That's good to hear. I bought this because I wanted you to see it."

"In that case, I want to get a better look."

At the moment, he was embracing her tightly from behind, so it was hard to see the front of the dress. He had caught a glimpse of it earlier, but he wanted to take a closer look.

At a word from Amane, Mahiru timidly turned her whole body around to face him and looked up at him with upturned eyes. She seemed a little uneasy.

He couldn't say whether she was nervous about being observed so closely or embarrassed to face him directly while sitting on the bed. But either way, he could tell she was feeling shy.

"…It looks great. Very cute."

"I—I know that. I know that you think I'm cute, Amane."

"Mm… This is going to sound embarrassing, but I think you're cuter than anyone else in the world."

Amane only had feelings for Mahiru, so for the time being, he had no intention of using the word *cute* to express his affection to anyone else. In the future, he might end up saying it to someone, but he wouldn't use it lightly.

Amane was being thoroughly genuine as he stroked Mahiru's cheek. Meanwhile, her eyes were darting all around the room.

"…Amane, you're being much more honest and bolder today."

"Because we're on a date. Even if it's a stay-at-home date."

The day before, Amane's father had really driven home that the boy ought to take the lead when he was on a date. Ultimately, they hadn't ended up going out, but the fact that they were having their date at home didn't change anything, so Amane figured he ought to seize the initiative.

When he tickled Mahiru's bright-red cheeks with his fingers, her face relaxed into a smile, and she cast a bashful gaze downward.

"…If you always came on this strongly, I don't think I could handle it," she said.

"Then should I make a habit of it to help you acclimate…?"

"Y-you can't… My heart won't be able to take it."

"Is it pounding that hard?"

"…It is."

Mahiru grabbed Amane's hand and pressed it right to the center of her chest.

Though it was only the back of his hand, her softness and warmth came through perfectly well. As did her strong heartbeat, no doubt quite a bit faster than usual.

He could feel its throbbing clearly through the thin fabric.

He held his breath and looked at Mahiru, and their eyes met.

In that moment, though her caramel-colored eyes were tearing up with embarrassment, she fixed her gaze on him as if she was about to make some sort of appeal.

"…It's unfair that your heart isn't pounding, too, Amane."

"…But it is. Very hard, in case you were wondering."

"Really?"

Mahiru buried her face in Amane's chest.

She probably did it partially to hide her shyness. But once she made out the rhythm of Amane's heart, throbbing loudly enough that even Amane could hear it, Mahiru murmured, looking pleased, "It really is."

"…Of course it's pounding. Look what my girlfriend's doing to me."

"But recently you've had this sort of…composure… It's not fair."

"But if I wasn't composed, I wouldn't seem very cool, would I?"

"That's not true. You're always cool, Amane."

"…Thanks very much."

He wanted to ask Mahiru whether she was saying that precisely because she knew it would make him lose his cool, but she probably really meant it, so he swallowed his words.

Instead, he squeezed her as she pressed against his chest and stroked her head.

"Damn, you're cute," he muttered quietly.

Mahiru lifted just the upper half of her face from Amane's chest and gave him a sheepish look. That glance alone brought intense feelings of affection surging out. It was obvious even to him that she really had him under her spell.

In a bid to regain some semblance of calm, Amane innocently patted and caressed Mahiru's head, and perhaps because her shyness had abated, she let him do it, seeming to enjoy herself.

Mahiru always appeared to like having her head patted, so maybe it helped her calm down.

"...Hey, Mahiru?"

"Yes?"

"I was thinking, if this is a date, that must mean that we're, like, always on a date, right? Since you're usually over at my place."

The reason Amane didn't feel like a stay-at-home date was an especially significant event was probably because he was used to having Mahiru around.

She was almost always there when he was spending time at home.

But they rarely ever flirted like they were doing now. Instead, they usually relaxed and chatted as they watched television, ate together, or studied—activities that didn't seem very date-like.

Perhaps that was why he hardly ever felt particularly nervous or excited.

"Heh-heh, good point. If this is all it is, I guess we're having stay-at-home dates every day, aren't we?"

"Maybe so. Though, I'd like to try going to your place instead of mine from time to time."

"To my apartment...?"

"Oh, I mean, I don't have any secret intentions. I guess I'm just curious."

Mahiru was usually, or rather *always* the one going to Amane's apartment, so he had a desire to reverse things and try visiting her place instead.

Though he had been inside it once before, on that occasion, he certainly hadn't been looking around. He was simply curious to see the place that Mahiru lived in, but when guys say they want to go into a girl's apartment, they tend to be suspected of ulterior motives.

That's why he'd never been able to voice the sentiment.

"I don't really mind," she said, "but...it's nothing special, you know?"

"I'm just curious... Also, there's something I wanted to check."

"What's that?"

"I just wanted to see what kind of picture of me you put in that frame on top of your desk."

Mahiru had mentioned the picture frame before.

He truly hadn't noticed it the one time he was in her apartment, so he'd been confused when she brought it up. But now that they were dating, he had figured it out.

She must have gone out of her way to confirm that he hadn't seen it because it was a picture of him.

From time to time, Mahiru, Itsuki, or Chitose would take his picture, so he had several candidates in mind, but he was curious which one it was.

"Wh-wha...?! Y-you knew about that?!"

"No, I just kind of figured it out after we started dating."

If he had known about the photo back then, he might have found his resolve a little sooner. A girl didn't normally keep a boy's photo displayed unless she really liked him, after all.

"...And y-you didn't find that creepy?"

"Why would it?"

"Depending on the circumstances, printing your photo and putting it up in my room kind of makes me sound like a stalker..."

"Hmm, that really does depend on the circumstances, though, doesn't it? If some stranger took a secret photo of me, I wouldn't really like that. But you're different. And anyway, you're probably the one who took it, either directly or by asking Itsuki or Chitose. That means I must have known it was being taken, and even if we weren't dating, I doubt I would be upset at you for displaying it... So seriously, which picture is it?"

"...One of you smiling. Mr. Akazawa took it for me, so it's a smile that I don't get to see..."

"So he's been slipping you stuff behind my back, huh?"

Amane was already aware that Itsuki and his girlfriend had been conspiring to support Mahiru, so he had no intention of reproaching his friend. But he was a little concerned that Itsuki might be sending her weird photos of him.

Convincing himself that Itsuki had at least enough good sense not to do that, Amane shrugged and said, "Well, that's fine then."

Mahiru let out an obvious sigh of relief.

"Thank goodness," she said. "I was wondering what I would do if you ended up hating me..."

"Think of it the other way around. How would you feel if I said I had a photo of you?"

"That would make me happy, but I would wonder about the composition and the picture quality... Oh, I see. So that's what this is about?"

"Exactly. But it doesn't sound like it's a weird photo, and you'll go bright red again if I keep harping on it, so I'll drop it for now."

If he teased her too much, Mahiru was likely to hug her knees and stop listening to him for a while. So he backed off meekly, though she seemed to guess why, glaring up at him with almost teary eyes.

But there was no blame in her gaze, probably because she was the one who had displayed his photo without permission.

Mahiru couldn't say anything more. Amane smiled slightly and patted her back to comfort her.

"But forgetting about all that, aren't you curious about your boyfriend's room?"

"I see your room quite often."

"It's true you come in to wake me up, and you've taken naps in my room, too."

Like he said, Mahiru entered Amane's bedroom on a fairly frequent basis.

Once he had come back home from a shopping trip and gone to his room to change clothes, only to see Mahiru sleeping there peacefully, causing him extreme consternation.

He had given her permission to go in, and there wasn't anything inside that he didn't want her to see. But he wished she would spare a thought about how her boyfriend would feel when he saw his girlfriend sleeping defenselessly in his own bed.

"I—I mean…your scent…is calming, and…"

"Well, it's not very calming for me. Normally, if a girl was sleeping in her boyfriend's bed, he would make a move on her."

"…What a gentleman you are."

"I'm happy that you trust me enough to let down your guard, but it's really testing my self-control, so please use some restraint."

"I'm sorry."

"…Next time, I'm holding a photo shoot of your sleeping face."

"D-don't do that."

"Then don't tempt me."

Mahiru didn't seem to especially object to the idea of him seeing her sleeping face, but she apparently hated the idea of him photographing it, a feeling he didn't really understand.

"To the best of my ability, I will limit my sleeping to times when I'm staying over," she said.

"…Okay."

When Mahiru shyly but happily mumbled those words, it reminded Amane that, although they hadn't decided what day yet, she had promised to stay over. Heat suddenly rose to his face.

He thought his reason might fail him if Mahiru was to lie down beside him dressed the way she was now. If she pressed against him and looked all bashful, he wasn't confident he could keep his hands off her.

"...I'd like to request that you wear extra-thick pajamas," he said.

"But it's so hot this time of year..."

"I won't know what to do."

"...You don't like frilly things?"

"If you don't care what happens to you, you can come over wearing whatever you like," he answered, implying that something might indeed happen if she did.

After staring intently up at him for a moment, Mahiru slowly smiled.

"If it's what you want, Amane, I'm all right with anything."

"...I know that, but—"

"Will you do something, then?"

"...Dammit! Now that you've made such a trusting statement, I can't."

Once she tilted her head and looked at him with that sweet, innocent expression, there was nothing he could do.

Of course, he hadn't been planning to do anything from the beginning, but he felt strangely frustrated, like he had been outmaneuvered.

"...I knew from the moment you gave me a warning that you had no intention to."

"Oh hush."

"Heh-heh. I think, overall, I've come out on top today. You're always pulling one over on me, but I won for once." Mahiru smiled impishly.

"Damn, you're cute," Amane answered, his words more praise than complaint, and lightly kissed the victor.

This alone was enough to turn Mahiru's face bright red, leaving her speechless and throwing her victory into question. She looked adorable.

"...That's no fair."

"What?"

"In the end, I always lose, don't I...?"

"That's not true. Let me have this one, since I lost to your charms long ago."

It simply wasn't true that Mahiru was always on the losing end of things. Amane was constantly done in by Mahiru's cuteness, and he wished she would occasionally yield him a victory.

"I guess there's no helping it, then...," she replied as she blushed and cast her eyes downward. Amane smiled slightly, happy that she'd given in to his argument.

Before Mahiru began to suspect that his smile came from a place of amusement, he hugged her closely, pressing her face into his chest.

Maybe that made her happy because she changed position slightly to snuggle against Amane, leaning into him.

He knew she was letting him pamper her like this precisely because she trusted him, and a heartwarming smile, different from the one a moment earlier, curled his lips.

"...You're quite clingy," he observed.

"You told me I could be."

"That's right. You can cling to me as much as you like."

"If I do that, I'll end up getting spoiled rotten, though..."

"You've already spoiled me rotten, so this is payback."

"I don't expect anything in return."

Mahiru raised her head and gave him a slightly dissatisfied look. In response, he planted a kiss on her lips, tenderly and gently this time. Her face lit up red with such energy that he could almost hear the sound of a gas stove lighting.

"…I get the feeling you think you can smooth over anything with a kiss," she said.

"You don't like it?"

"I don't dislike it, but… Hmm."

He heard her grumble quietly about how it wasn't fair, before grinding her forehead into his chest. Amane smiled and carefully tidied up her slightly disheveled hair with his fingers.

He combed through it with his hand, and it was soon back in order. Her smooth, glossy, straight hair was extremely pleasant to touch, and once he'd fixed it, he couldn't help touching it some more. Mahiru didn't seem to dislike it—in fact, it was putting her in a good mood, so he had no reason to stop.

As he stroked her head, he imagined he was petting a cat in his lap. Mahiru must have been totally relaxed, and she nuzzled her face up against Amane's body.

"…I'm so happy," she said. "It's wonderful to spend a leisurely, relaxing time at your house like this."

"I'm glad to hear it. I was worried about whether you would enjoy yourself, coming here."

"Heh-heh, I'm enjoying myself so much that I'm reluctant to go back."

Before the trip, Amane had puzzled over what he would do if Mahiru didn't settle in at his home, or if she felt uncomfortable, but apparently there had been no need to worry.

"Seems like you've really settled in."

"It's all thanks to your parents being so hospitable."

"They've been treating you with more affection than they give me."

"Are you pouting?"

"I'm not pouting."

He had known perfectly well that his parents were going to pay more attention to Mahiru, even before they arrived, and Mahiru had been making an effort not to leave Amane's side, so he wasn't feeling peevish about it anymore.

He did think that his parents were coming on a little too strong, clearly expecting her to eventually become their daughter-in-law. But they had been waiting a long time for a girl like her to enter his life, so he understood how they felt.

"Heh-heh, are you sure, Amane? If you started pouting, I'd have to squeeze you tight."

"Are you saying you won't if I'm not pouting?"

"No. For you, Amane, I'll do it anytime."

"All right then, can I take you up on that?"

"Go ahead."

Mahiru stopped leaning against Amane for a moment and spread her arms out toward him. He clamped his lips shut, unsure of what to do. She was probably telling him to leap right in.

Even under normal circumstances, Mahiru had a well-balanced figure that stuck out where it was supposed to stick out and curved in where it was supposed to curve in. But now she was wearing an off-the-shoulder dress. He knew he would likely find heaven if he buried his face against her, but he was worried about any possible jiggling.

But you're her boyfriend, so that ought to be fine..., whispered a little devil inside him. *It'll be okay as long as you don't do anything; she'll forgive you for enjoying yourself.*

Amane groaned quietly at the desires that threatened to unsettle him.

He couldn't resist the bewitching temptation.

He put his arms around Mahiru's back and buried his face in her exposed cleavage.

If he shifted his face down slightly, he would end up plunging straight into those soft swells. Naturally, at his current level of endurance, he could never go that far. But he brought his lips to her beautiful collarbone and smooth, flawless pale skin and got his fill of her faintly sweet scent.

Mahiru seemed a little ticklish but showed no signs of discomfort. Rather, she happily wrapped her arms around Amane and embraced him in return. She patted his back like someone doting on a child.

"Heh-heh, you're clingy, too, Amane."

"Hush, you."

"It's fine, go ahead and touch all you want. I'll spoil you silly."

"You already have."

He felt like she was causing him to melt into goo—and that he was melting her in return. It seemed they had reached the stage where they were spoiling each other so much they were fusing together until neither of them could survive alone.

He looked up at Mahiru while lightly kissing the fresh expanse of her décolletage, and she giggled and continued embracing him. She seemed to be enjoying herself.

"When we sit like this, you seem smaller, Amane. Usually you feel big and sturdy."

"Do I...? You're so small and thin, Mahiru. I can easily wrap you up in my arms."

"But right now you're the one being wrapped up... You know, maybe I'm so small specifically so you can fit me in your arms."

"Are you saying you were made for me, Mahiru?"

"Yes... And you, me."

"Mm."

"Heh-heh."

She smiled and caressed him comfortingly. Amane was nearly at his limit. He shifted and moved up slightly to kiss her neck.

She reacted quickly with a little jolt—her neck must be sensitive.

He already knew her ears were a weak spot, and now he realized her neck was, too.

"Nn... Be sure not to leave any marks, please."

"I won't, but I *will* kiss you."

"Th-that tickles; I can't take it..."

"If you don't like it, you can always push me away."

"...Don't be mean."

He could hear a sulking tone in her voice, as if to say, *You know I wouldn't do that.* But he was confident that if she truly disliked it, she would stop him, so there was no problem.

After Amane had lightly kissed her skin for a little while, Mahiru started slapping at his back like she wanted him to stop, so he left it there.

Mahiru's cheeks were flushed red, as if she was roasting from the inside. She glared at him, so he embraced her and stroked her head to calm her down.

"...We got a little sidetracked, but you were saying you didn't want to go back?"

If he kept up at the current pace, she would definitely get peevish with him, so Amane tried to return to their earlier conversation.

After staring blankly for a moment, Mahiru flashed him an easygoing smile.

"No, that's not it... I'll just be a little lonely, I guess."

"That's good to hear."

"Huh?"

"Well, it means you've been very comfortable here, right?"

"Th-that's true, but—"

"You could come with me again next time. At the end of the year, or next summer, maybe."

After this trip, Amane was sure to visit his parents again. He had originally been told to show his face twice a year, during the long breaks in summer and winter. So if it was all right with Mahiru, they could make the trip together.

His parents would both be delighted, and Amane wouldn't have to be away from Mahiru for a long stretch of time.

"...Again..."

"You don't want to?"

"Th-that's not what I said."

"...You know you can think of this place as your own home, right?"

"...Okay."

He had whispered the invitation, hoping to give Mahiru somewhere she could call home. In return, she didn't even try to hide the joy welling up inside her. Putting on a sweet smile, she buried her face in Amane's shoulder.

Chapter 5

One More Farewell

It's often said that clear weather always comes after a typhoon, and that is precisely what happened. When the relentless driving rain stopped, and the threatening dark-gray clouds disappeared, they left behind blue skies.

"If only it had passed us one day earlier, we could have gone on our date," Amane mumbled, gazing out the living room window at the fine, summer weather—a complete change from the day before.

Mahiru was beside him, gazing out the window in the same way, and he could see her reflection smile slightly.

"Oh well," she said. "We can't do anything about the past, and I'm satisfied as long as you're by my side. The space next to me is always open for you, Amane, so we can go out another time."

"And I'm grateful, but you know... You say you hold a space for me, but sometimes Chitose butts in and takes it."

"Consider Chitose a special case."

Mahiru laughed elegantly, and Amane lightly shrugged in response.

Chitose certainly seemed to be an exception in Mahiru's book. Their personalities were nothing alike, but the other girl appeared to be having a good influence on Mahiru, who had taken a real liking to the carefree Chitose.

Amane wasn't sure how their friendship had developed while he wasn't around, but it hadn't been long before the girls formed a much tighter bond than he had expected.

That was a good thing, but Chitose sometimes had a strange influence on Mahiru that he wasn't sure he liked.

"Heh-heh, are you getting jealous of girls, too?" Mahiru teased.

"I'm not that petty, you know. It's just, well, I've got some mixed feelings about you two being so close."

"Heh-heh… I owe a lot to Chitose, so you'll have to allow it."

"It's not a question of allowing it. I don't have any intention of telling you what you can and can't do. I trust you."

Even though he was her boyfriend, he naturally had no plans to interfere with her friendships. To his way of thinking, asking her things like how close she was with Chitose and what they talked about would be an infringement on her privacy.

"I trust you, too, Amane… Even if you were to make some female friends, I wouldn't get mad."

"You think I'm capable of that…?"

"I think that, as you are now, you're entirely capable of building normal, friendly relationships."

"You do?"

It was true that, after Amane began dating Mahiru, the girls in his class had started coming up to talk to him, and he didn't think he'd messed up too badly during any of those interactions. But he'd only just started having normal interactions with his classmates.

Mahiru was probably right to call those friendly relationships, but the distance between Amane and his classmates was still wide enough that he wouldn't call them friends.

Obviously, the only person who Amane could call a friend of the opposite sex was Chitose, and he wasn't inclined to go out of his way to make any others.

To Amane, it was more important to cherish the relationships he currently had, and though he might become close with other people in the process, he wasn't planning to put in special effort to actively enlarge his circle of friends.

"Come to think of it, you don't seem to have the slightest inclination to make friends with girls," Mahiru pointed out.

"Why would I do something that could be misunderstood by my girlfriend...? You might not get angry, but I know you'd be quietly jealous."

"Hmph. I'm pretty open-minded, you know."

"I can see, you know, looking-worried tears in your eyes."

Mahiru understood that Amane would never do anything that could be misconstrued as cheating, and Amane was fully aware of how much she trusted him.

Be that as it may, Amane also knew it would bring Mahiru a certain discomfort to see another girl by his side.

She probably wouldn't suspect Amane of anything, but it was clear that she wouldn't like it, so Amane was going to do his best not to upset her.

"I'm not going to do anything that might be misunderstood."

"...I know."

He reassured her, dead serious, and Mahiru mumbled bashfully in response. Then she head-butted his upper arm. Though he understood she was trying to hide her embarrassment, he didn't point that out and let her do as she pleased.

Quietly gazing at the blue sky out the window, he waited for Mahiru to calm down.

"...We only have a little while longer to enjoy this scenery," he murmured quietly.

Mahiru, having tucked away her embarrassment, raised her head and looked at him. Amane turned to gaze back at her. It must have occurred to her that their stay was about to come to an end because she answered with a hint of regret, "We're leaving tomorrow already, huh?"

They had packed a lot of vacation into this homecoming, but it felt like they'd been there a much shorter time than they actually had, perhaps because so many things had happened so quickly.

"Once we leave, it'll be a while before we come back," Amane said. "I'm a little reluctant to go."

"Me too; it feels sad to say good-bye so soon, now that I finally got to spend so much time with your parents. Especially after all they've done for me."

"I have a feeling they were just doing whatever they wanted…"

"Heh-heh, and that was perfect as far as I'm concerned."

He thought back on how his parents had doted on Mahiru even more than their own son, and her happiness at the gesture in turn filled him with joy.

There was a part of Mahiru that, considering her home situation, had been longing to find a happy family, so Amane was glad he and his parents had been able to fulfill that desire. He was hesitant to call them a substitute family, but if Mahiru had gotten even a little bit of warmth out of visiting the Fujimiya household, he was glad.

"I guess it's almost time to say good-bye to this place," Mahiru muttered. "I was hesitant to walk around an unfamiliar place alone, so the only time I went outside was when I was with you and your family, but I wish I could have seen a bit more of it."

"In that case, do you want to go for a walk?"

Their previous attempt had been cut off halfway through due to the appearance of Toujou, so Mahiru hadn't gotten much of a chance to look around.

That reunion itself had ended up being a good thing, but their walk had been left unfinished.

"I-is that all right? Just because of my selfish desire…"

"Why would you call it selfish? It's just a walk. I've been planning to go out and take a last look around anyway."

He'd intended the little stroll more for his own refreshment than for Mahiru's sake, but there was no problem with including her.

In fact, he was happy to be able to continue their walk from the other day.

In response to Amane's welcoming attitude, Mahiru blinked dramatically, then smiled slightly, a little embarrassed.

"All right, let's go. We can only stay a little longer, and since we made the trip, I want to see more of the city where you grew up."

"Last time was a little eventful, after all."

"…I'm glad you're not letting it bother you, Amane."

"Like I told you, it's all in the past now."

"I know, but—"

"Even if I was hurt, I have a feeling that you would heal me."

"…If you'll let me, I'll heal you and spoil you as much as you like!"

"Be careful. If you pamper me that much, I really will end up spoiled rotten."

Recently, even Amane could see that he was shaping up well. But if Mahiru made a serious effort at pampering him, he wouldn't be able to resist falling victim to her temptations.

He had gone to such pains to discipline himself, and he wanted to avoid having it all dissolved away in a single stroke by Mahiru.

"At the moment, you're doing quite well, so I think a little spoiling is in order."

"What exactly is your goal here, Mahiru?"

"To offer specially tailored comfort, just for you, Amane."

She looked at him with a broad, innocent grin, so was it only his own wicked mind that sensed something alluring and sensual behind her expression?

He wanted to be pampered and healed, and he felt like she saw right through him to all of those desires he was keeping deep inside.

He turned away from her.

"...Right."

"Feeling shy?"

"Quit it. Look, I'm going to go get ready."

"Heh-heh, okaaay!" Mahiru answered cheerfully. She seemed pleased that she had gotten her revenge for earlier.

Amane looked away, gently biting the inside of his cheek as he tried not to make a face.

Amane wasn't wearing anything particularly special, so he was ready to leave right away, but the same did not apply to Mahiru.

After changing into outdoor clothes, she diligently smeared herself with sunscreen to ward off UV rays. Apparently, if she didn't take such measures, she would basically burn immediately, and her skin would turn red and start to peel. So she applied sunscreen with quite a bit of care.

He was leisurely watching her when Mahiru held out the tube of sunscreen to him and demanded, "You too, Amane," with a reproachful look.

He accepted her kindness without protest.

"...I think you ought to be a little more careful, Amane. Even if you've got tough skin, the sun's rays are strong."

"Well, I'm tanner than I was before I started going outside, and it's not healthy to be too pale, so I think I'm okay..."

"A sunburn is a real burn, and there's no use in getting burned if you don't have to. Even if you do tan, you don't need to expose yourself to such strong sunlight. If it gets bad enough, your skin can even blister."

©Hanekoto

The sun's rays weren't especially bright that day, but the sky was completely clear. Mahiru carefully applied sunscreen on Amane's face, insisting it was better to be safe than sorry.

With his eyes closed, Amane replied, "I get it. I get it."

While Mahiru was applying his sunscreen, she took the opportunity to play with his face a little. Once she seemed satisfied, Amane took Mahiru by the hand, and they went outside.

The moment they stepped through the door, they were struck by the withering heat. Amane was once again impressed by the power of air conditioning—one of civilization's greatest tools.

It shouldn't have been a surprise, considering it was afternoon at the height of summer, but it was sweltering. Even though Amane was wearing a hat, the sun was still dazzling, and he could feel the intensity of its fiery rays threatening to scorch his skin.

"It sure is hot, huh?"

Wearing a straw hat and arm covers, and carrying a small parasol, Mahiru was thoroughly protected from sunburn, but Amane was worried that she might feel the heat more since she was smaller.

"Should we pull a U-turn?" he asked.

"No. This is our precious final outing here, and I want to enjoy it," Mahiru replied. "…Will you be all right without a parasol, Amane?"

"I've got some shopping to do on the way home, so it'll be one more thing to carry, and I figure I'll be all right getting some sun if it's just today."

If Amane walked beside Mahiru while carrying a parasol of his own, there was a possibility that they would bump each other, and if the two of them walked side by side, they might be a nuisance to other pedestrians.

Amane wasn't as worried about sunburn as Mahiru was, so he decided it was all right to go without. After all, she had been kind enough to apply his sunscreen.

Besides, Mahiru was probably happy that he had left one hand free.

When he smoothly squeezed her palm, Mahiru looked at him. He pretended not to notice anything and asked her, "What's up?"

But after casting her eyes downward, looking a little embarrassed, Mahiru slowly shook her head.

He decided not to mention that the dapple of sunshine passing through her parasol was dancing on her face. Without pausing, Amane smiled faintly, tugged on Mahiru's hand, and started walking. "We went the opposite direction last time, but no matter which way we go, there's nothing too interesting."

They might be going a different way than their last outing, but since Amane's house was in a quiet residential neighborhood, there weren't any particularly notable shops or points of interest nearby.

As they walked, they passed typical houses and convenience stores, and a few small playgrounds, but nothing that seemed like it would delight Mahiru.

Nevertheless, she seemed to be finding the scenery more novel than Amane would have expected, and her downcast caramel-colored eyes appeared to be sparkling brightly.

"Oh really?" she said. "I think it's fun just to stroll around exploring unfamiliar places. Like when I take a look in a grocery store somewhere I've never been before. It's fun to see how their lineup of products differs from what the store in my neighborhood has."

"How should I say this? It sounds like you have a real eye for the small stuff. Though, I guess things change when you cross into another prefecture, so it can be fun to look for those differences."

"Heh-heh. I like to see what kinds of things are cheap in certain areas, and what's for sale, and so on. I always want to buy local products when I see them."

"Do you want to go in and buy something?"

Since she'd made such a point of it, he suddenly wanted to show Mahiru the local produce. Conveniently, there was a supermarket nearby, so he pointed it out, but Mahiru shook her head slowly.

"No, it's not a good idea to add something else to carry right at the start of our walk. Besides, if we have to use our hands to carry it…"

She seemed to struggle to get the words out, and her voice rapidly grew quiet. He could tell what Mahiru was thinking, so he tickled her palm with his fingers.

"…I'll be sure to leave one hand open, okay?"

"I-it's fine. I'd prefer you unencumbered for now, so I can cling to you as I please."

"Okay."

If that's what Mahiru wanted, then any further discussion was pointless.

Musing on how adorable she was, clinging tightly to him while taking care not to hit him with her parasol, Amane decided to let Mahiru do as she wished.

Though passersby kept looking at them, Amane wasn't particularly bothered. The two of them were always showered with attention whenever he went out walking with Mahiru.

He made eye contact with one of his mother's acquaintances who happened to live in the neighborhood, but when he smiled and gave a little bow, she seemed to decide it was best not to interfere and didn't come over to talk to them. He was a little irritated, knowing she would report it back to his mother later, but there was nothing he could do about it.

Besides, by the time his mother heard anything, they would likely already be on their way back, so there was no harm in it.

Putting on a rather proper expression, he tugged at Mahiru's hand. She looked up at him questioningly. "Is something the matter?" she asked.

"Nope, nothing at all. Actually, my old elementary school is right over here."

If he mentioned his mother's friend to Mahiru, it seemed likely that she would ask if they should go say hello. So partially to avoid that conversation, he found a notable building in the direction they were traveling and directed Mahiru toward it.

Mahiru had said she wanted to see where Amane had spent his time, so the elementary school fit the bill perfectly.

After making sure he had captured Mahiru's interest, Amane shifted his gaze over to his alma mater. Through the fence, he could see children playing in the schoolyard, which seemed to have been left open for students during the break.

He hadn't been there for four years, but as far as he could see from the outside, not much had changed from how he remembered it. About the only difference he noticed was a sign reading ENTRY PRO-HIBITED hanging on a section of deteriorating playground equipment.

"We can't go in, since we're not students, but I used to run around like that with my friends, a long time ago."

"You were a rowdy little kid when you were in elementary school, weren't you, Amane?"

"I don't know if I was rowdy exactly, but I think I was pretty energetic. I wasn't as much of a shut-in as I am now, at least. I liked playing inside, too, but I spent time outside with my friends and went to all sorts of places with my mom and dad."

In his elementary school days, Amane had been a healthy, normal child. He ate well, laughed a lot, and played all the time. He ran around innocently with neighborhood children and got scolded for coming home with his clothes covered in mud. These days, it was difficult to imagine what a carefree kid he had been.

"It's hard to believe, looking at you now," said Mahiru, sounding amused. She must have been thinking the same thing.

Amane's mouth tensed up a little bit, and he gently massaged her hand in retaliation. "I think it's good that I had a phase like that... Because now, aside from when I go exercise, I prefer to spend my time relaxing at home. And I've only got a few friends who invite me to hang out."

"Actually, though I have a lot of friends, I don't know many of them that well. So the number of people I actually spend time with is pretty small, too."

Mahiru told him this readily, without any self-deprecation. Amane knew that, despite her wide circle of friends, she was the type who hardly let anyone inside her shell.

Precisely because she acted as the school's "angel," she did not have deep friendships. Instead, she formed only loose connections with all their classmates, who saw her as a perfect girl to be admired by everyone.

Now that angel mask was slipping a little, and she was beginning to let the girls in their class see her honest, shy side.

In fact, Mahiru was becoming even more popular, probably because she'd begun to lose her intimidatingly perfect image as a girl who was kind to everyone but who didn't let anyone get close.

"Recently, though, you've been hanging out with other girls together with Chitose, right? I bet it's because you've gotten more approachable."

"W-well, I'd be happy if that was true, but... They ask me a lot about our relationship, so it's kind of difficult."

"...You're not telling them anything weird, right?"

When Mahiru got used to someone, she would occasionally let her mouth run without thinking, so he hoped she was being careful about what information she shared. She frequently let things leak to Chitose, and Amane had been embarrassed before.

"I'm not close enough to anyone to talk openly like that, and of course, I would be embarrassed to speak of certain things… Though, Chitose is an exception," she admitted.

"So you've been talking to Chitose, huh?"

"J-just a little bit; I haven't told her everything."

"Oh reeeally?"

"R-really!"

Mahiru was getting flustered, which made him a little suspicious, but he knew it wouldn't be good to question her too persistently. Instead, he answered with a smile, "Well, that's good, but I'm a little worried how much is 'a little bit.' I trust you to decide what's okay to talk about, though."

"…So you're saying you haven't told Mr. Akazawa anything?"

She gave him an accusatory look, but Amane didn't have anything to feel guilty about.

"Not really, but that's because I know he'd only complain about me bragging or tease me."

Amane was the type of person who didn't ask advice about big things, or if he did, he would speak with purposeful ambiguity, so as not to reveal too much information. It wasn't because he was secretive, but because he was embarrassed.

"…I feel like I'm being criticized here," Mahiru said.

"I'm not criticizing, honest. And in your case, I bet you mostly let things slip while you're asking for advice."

"…I'm not sure I like how well you know me."

"It's a habit of yours, you know."

He often heard stories from Chitose that started with "Mahiru told me—" so he knew well from personal experience that Mahiru was always carelessly revealing things. He wasn't trying to criticize her for it, but he got embarrassed if she said too much, so if possible, he wished she would limit what she shared.

Amane gave her a look that said *Be careful, okay?* and Mahiru pouted, looking a little dissatisfied. In response, Amane flashed her a faint smile, then tugged at her hand.

"Don't make that face... Come on, let's go."

People might wonder what they were doing if they stood around for too long in front of the elementary school.

Mahiru obediently followed him, but she still looked unhappy, so he reached over with his free hand and gently patted her head. The way her eyes scrunched up made it seem like it tickled.

He went on to gently stroke her cheek, noticing that she was warmer than usual. Though he assumed it was because they were outside, he instinctively put his whole hand against her forehead and checked her temperature.

"You're kind of warm; are you feeling all right?"

"Huh? Yes, I've got no signs of heatstroke. My body temperature is up because it's so hot. Actually, you seem more likely to overheat, Amane. I've got a parasol, but you only have a hat."

She put her hand under his bangs and touched his forehead, asking if *he* was doing all right. But Amane's body temperature had always been on the high side, so she probably couldn't tell anything from simply touching him.

After putting her hand against his slightly sweaty skin, Mahiru smiled and said, "I feel like you're running a little hot, too, Amane. I think it would be best for both of us to take a little break. We're out here in the sweltering heat, after all."

"For sure... Should we stop holding hands?"

They had been doing so the whole time, and he lifted up their palms without letting go to ask what they should do. Mahiru didn't try to let go, either; instead, she adjusted her fingers to hold on even tighter.

"Th-the thing is: I don't want to let go yet."

"I'm sweaty, though."

"…Is it unpleasant?"

"No, as long as you're not uncomfortable, it's fine. All right, there's a café over there, so let's hold hands just until we get there, okay? …People will stare if we don't let go inside, after all."

If they kept touching each other like this inside the café, they were guaranteed to get stares that said *Do that somewhere else,* so he decided to be reasonable.

And yet Mahiru squeezed his hand even tighter, as if to tell him not to let go, so he began to wonder if something was wrong.

"…Is something the matter?"

"No, just… Normally, I run colder than you, so now that we're about the same temperature, touching you like this feels like we're melting and blending together. It's nice."

"…Mahiru, you can never say that around anyone else."

"Huh? Why are you saying that, all of a sudden?"

"Look, it's okay now, but you're really playing with fire."

He knew that Mahiru had absolutely no such intentions, but it was a dangerous remark that could be taken to imply something else. Amane started walking again, pulling the confused Mahiru along with some force in order to keep her quiet.

Though his attitude was a little insistent, Mahiru was glued to his side, and for some reason, she seemed even happier than before. As he watched her, he feared he might succumb to a heatstroke of a different kind.

"…Oh, look, Amane. It says there's a fireworks festival."

After taking a brief break at the café and then wandering around the area for a little while, they headed home. On the way, Mahiru spotted a flier on a telephone pole and pointed it out cheerily.

The flier wasn't very dirty or torn, so it had probably been posted recently. The gist of it was that the large shopping district nearby was putting on a summer festival and fireworks exhibition.

In elementary school, Amane had gone to the event nearly every year, but he didn't remember going after he started middle school. He hadn't had the emotional bandwidth for it, and he would have felt embarrassed to go with his parents, a reason that now seemed almost cute.

"Now that you mention it, summer festivals and fireworks displays are starting up all over the place," Amane remarked. "I saw something about it on TV."

Amane was filled with nostalgia as he read the details on the flier. However, he realized that the event would be held after they were already back in their respective apartments.

"That's too bad," Mahiru said. "The summer festival here will happen after we've gone home."

"Nothing we can do about that," he said, shrugging. "Did you want to go to the festival?"

"I've never been to one before, so I'd like to go sometime. But if the timing doesn't work, there's not much we can do. Besides, it's enough for me just to be with you, even if we don't go to a festival."

"You've gotta stop it with those surprise attacks!"

Amane knew that Mahiru liked to be with him, but when she said it out loud, as if it was the most natural thing in the world, he couldn't help but feel embarrassed.

"I can't," she said. "In my heart, I'm always by your side."

"…I know that, but come on."

"Heh-heh!"

Mahiru giggled, looking delighted that Amane was flustered. He shut his mouth in frustration and stared at the flier again.

Fireworks exhibitions and summer festivals were generally pretty similar no matter where they were held. And events in different prefectures were even less concerned about overlapping programming.

There ought to be one or two summer festivals happening around where they lived as well. Amane made a mental note to look up information after they got back—and to have his mother send some *yukata* along with their luggage.

He didn't want to disappoint Mahiru, so he intended to bring it up with her after checking to make sure there was a festival with a decent program they could attend and clearing his schedule. As he walked leisurely back toward his parents' house, he tried to etch these plans into his mind so he wouldn't forget them.

Suddenly, he heard a childish voice gasp. He didn't know where the voice had come from, so he stopped, wondering what was going on. Just then, something crashed right into his abdomen. A shrill gasp of surprise came from beside him in Mahiru's familiar voice.

The impact wasn't strong enough to knock him over, and when Amane, stiff from shock, looked cautiously down, he saw a child with her head buried in his belly.

"Big Brother Amane!"

A face he recognized popped up to look at him, and along with his surprise, an awkward smile sprang to his lips.

"Oh, Hanada's little sister? It's been a while. You seem well."

He would have been quite bewildered if the child had been a stranger, but his wariness evaporated at the sight of her familiar face. He knew her, though she was much taller than he remembered.

The little girl, who seemed to be about nine or ten, responded to Amane's words with a childlike smile.

Beside Amane, Mahiru was failing to hide her confusion at the unfamiliar girl embracing her boyfriend, and her hand holding Amane's grew tense.

"Um, Amane, who is this?"

"Oh, sorry if she surprised you. This girl is my childhood friend's...well, we weren't that close, but anyway, she's the little sister of a classmate I've known for a long time. We used to play together a lot."

To be more precise, that classmate had insisted on bringing her along to play with them. But Amane didn't mind spending time with younger children, so he'd played with her regularly. Since they were seven years apart in age, he had felt responsible for taking care of her.

His connection to the girl had mostly disappeared after he lost touch with her brother, so it had been a long time since he had even spoken to her.

"You never come back to see us, Amane! It's been so long!"

"Sorry, I've been pretty busy," he said. "Actually, I'm surprised you recognized me after all this time."

"I'd know you anywhere; you're like a big brother to me. Even from far away, I was like, 'That's gotta be Amane!'"

"You've got a good eye. Hey, wait a second, don't hug me like that."

She had probably been about seven years old the last time he saw her, but her energy and high spirits hadn't changed at all. She was embracing him, innocently of course, but it put him in a bit of a fix since his girlfriend was standing right beside them.

Amane felt confident that Mahiru wouldn't think he was cheating, but it was still possible that she might find it objectionable. When he cautiously looked over at her, she still seemed taken aback.

"I hope this isn't giving you the wrong idea or anything."

"O-of course not, Amane. I know you're not that sort of person. But...I was very surprised."

There was nothing he could do about the situation, so if Mahiru had misunderstood, he was afraid he'd simply have to explain and apologize. But even Mahiru seemed to realize that Amane would never look at an elementary schooler that way.

Still, she couldn't hide her bewilderment at how much the girl adored him.

The Hanada girl looked disappointed when Amane gently pried her off of him, but then she belatedly noticed Mahiru's presence beside him, and her big eyes got even rounder.

"Big Brother Amane, do you know this girl?"

"Um," Mahiru started. "I'm…"

"She's my girlfriend," answered Amane.

He didn't beat around the bush, figuring that the child was at an age where she could understand, and the girl's round eyes opened so wide they looked like they might fall out of her head.

"Girlfriend…like a sweetheart?"

"Yep. She's my sweetheart, and she's very important to me."

He introduced Mahiru in a way that would be easiest to understand, and her cheeks flushed, perhaps out of embarrassment after Amane openly called her his sweetheart.

Despite this, Mahiru leaned over a little and greeted the girl with a cheery smile, "Nice to meet you."

The young girl froze for a moment but eventually seemed to understand. She looked like she might topple over.

"N-no way… Amane has a sweetheart…?"

"Why are you so surprised…?"

"I mean, my big brother has never brought home a girl…and he said that you guys were two of a kind…"

"It's all up to fate, I guess."

It seemed Amane had been conscripted into a company of guys who couldn't get girlfriends without his knowledge.

Amane and Mahiru had nearly made it back to Amane's parents' house, and that meant they were also near his former friend's house, which was in the same neighborhood. Thinking about it, it was perfectly reasonable that they'd run into his friend's little sister. They might easily have run into his former friend himself.

"How is your big brother? Is he well?"

"He's fine. He's out right now, but I think he'll be coming back before too long."

"Oh, is that right?"

Amane felt a little relieved, not because he was a negative guy who didn't want to see his old friend, but because he was still struggling to work out how he should act around him.

His friend's younger sister stared intently up at Amane, with a troubled look on her young face. It was like she could see right through him.

"...Do you still hate my big brother?"

Amane didn't know what her brother had told her, but she seemed to think that Amane had come to hate him.

"I never hated him," he said.

They had simply drifted apart—that was probably the best way to put it.

Amane didn't hate the other boy or bear any sort of grudge against him.

It was just that their minds had settled and cleared, and as a result, their connection had grown too distant and substanceless to be considered a friendship.

They had mutually dissolved their bond—that felt like an accurate way to describe it.

Back then, Hanada had prioritized his own safety. Rather than extend a helping hand to the friendless Amane, he had chosen to avoid being ostracized as well.

It was a completely reasonable choice. A school's social circle is small, and it's difficult to resist the current of popular opinion.

Besides, back then, even if someone had extended a helping hand, Amane probably would have rejected it. He hadn't been able to trust anybody. In his insecurity, he probably would have said something terrible and hurt the other boy before severing ties with him anyway.

So the fact that their relationship had dissolved gradually wasn't a bad thing. They hadn't broken it off out of spite; it had simply come undone. That was all there was to it.

"So then, will you make up with him?"

"I'm not sure; it depends on how he feels. But I don't think it'll change anything, and I doubt we'll go back to how we were."

He answered her honestly, reasoning that it would only make her sad later if he lied, and she frowned.

Amane didn't plan on taking back what he'd said.

Even if the boys did apologize to each other, the relationship they'd had before their estrangement would never be the same. Even if you tie a cut string back together, it will never return to how it was. The knot of lingering discomfort will always be visible.

Even if they pretended not to see it, the friendship would most likely fade away again or break apart.

Hanada's younger sister looked like she wanted to say something, but before she could, her gaze shifted to look behind him.

"Kaname, who are you talking to…?"

Amane turned around and saw a face from the past.

The two friends hadn't quarreled or anything, so when Amane shifted his gaze to look at the other boy, he got a somewhat awkward greeting in return.

"…Long time no see."

It was easy to tell that Hanada felt uncomfortable, so Amane smiled in spite of himself. "Been a while, huh?" he said. "Maybe two or three years since we've really talked. Glad to see you're doing well."

"That's my line…," Hanada replied. "You look better than I expected."

"Well, I am doing pretty well. Physically, I'm much healthier than I was way back when."

"Wow, now you're just bragging. Then again, you used to be so lanky you looked like a skeleton."

"That wasn't really my fault."

"...No, it wasn't."

Hanada's mood inevitably turned gloomy when he thought about the past. Amane shrugged, then glanced over at Mahiru.

They were probably about to broach some topics Hanada's younger sister shouldn't hear, but it would be difficult to get Mahiru to lead her away.

"Kaname, go show this lady our garden. And make sure to show off Mom's flower beds. You know how she's always complaining that no one comes to see them."

"Do you have something to talk about with Amane, Big Brother?"

"That's right, we've got to talk man-to-man."

Hanada's little sister seemed to understand that the two boys had something they wanted to discuss. She frowned a little, then said "Okay!" and took Mahiru by the hand. "Come on, Miss, it's just over there."

Mahiru must have been paying attention, too. She obediently let herself be led away.

"S-see you later...Amane."

"Yeah, see you later."

After they were alone, Hanada forced himself to smile.

"Is she your girlfriend?" he asked.

"Yeah, she is. We came here together."

"Imagine, Amane getting a girlfriend. I guess you never know what might happen, huh?"

"Sounds like you didn't think very highly of me."

"I mean, the way you looked the last time I saw you, there'd be no way."

The last time they had seen each other face-to-face would have been at their middle school graduation ceremony, though they hadn't spoken. Amane had recovered somewhat by then, but even so, he'd probably looked lifeless.

"Seems like things are working out in the city."

"Yeah, thanks to everyone's support."

"Do I detect sarcasm?"

"Why would you?"

"…Because things didn't end well between us."

His former friend's words were bitter. But Amane felt no bitterness rise up inside himself.

"That's true. But I don't blame you for any of it," he said. "I just happened to run into you while I was back. I didn't come to see you on purpose, and I hope I'm not bothering you."

Honestly, Amane didn't resent Hanada. He wasn't mad at him, and he didn't blame him for what happened. His emotions remained level as they spoke.

But he couldn't stop the confusion showing on his face as he realized that Hanada was more worried about the past than he was. Amane was the one who had been hurt, after all. Being worried over made him feel awkward, and he wished Hanada would stop fretting about it.

"…Seeing you so unfazed makes me think I'm the weird one," Hanada said.

"Yeah man, you *are* weird. Stop letting it get to you. I bet you'd forgotten all about it until you saw my face, right? It's no big deal."

"Are you making a self-deprecating joke?"

"No way. If you look at it objectively, stuff like that happens all the time. It's only important to the person it's happening to. I'm just stating facts, I didn't mean to make a dig at you. Sorry."

"It doesn't feel right for you to be apologizing; I'm the one who should be saying sorry."

"I wouldn't know how to react if you did that. I don't remember you doing anything worth apologizing for, Hanada."

"I didn't do anything at all; that's the problem."

"I think it's because you didn't do anything that I didn't try to push you away... Anyway, it was a long time ago, so you don't need to feel bad about it."

Amane knew that if his friend had extended a half-hearted helping hand, he probably would have rejected it, and a rift would have opened between them. Instead, because he had quietly kept his distance, the friendship had died out naturally.

Amane didn't get worked up or feel hurt; he simply stated the facts in a lighthearted way.

Hanada shot him a deflated grin. "...I see; so for you, it's already in the past."

"Yeah," Amane said, nodding. "I ran into Toujou, too, and realized I was already over it. I think everything turned out all right in the end."

"You've gotten stronger in more ways than one, haven't you? ...I bet Toujou hasn't changed a bit. I'm in high school with him, so I know."

"I was actually surprised by how little he'd changed. I guess it depends on the person whether that's a good or a bad thing."

Whether change was positive varied from person to person. Remaining the same could also be the right choice.

Amane had changed because he had wanted to. If it hadn't been necessary, he would have been all right staying the same. It seemed like Toujou felt no need to change.

Hanada shrugged. "...You really don't seem bothered by it." He sounded surprised that Amane could talk about someone so intimately connected to the troubles of his past in such an easy manner.

"That's because I've found closure. Though, Toujou didn't seem too pleased about it."

"I bet he was furious. Try not to provoke him too much."

"Why do you assume I provoked him? He was the one doing the provoking."

"With that attitude, I wouldn't be surprised if he lashed out at you."

"Well, he didn't seem happy, but that was the end of it."

"What if you run into him again?"

"I don't have any intention to see him ever again. It definitely wouldn't be any fun for me. Besides, I hardly ever have reason to come back here."

It didn't make much sense to go out of his way to see someone he'd left in the past. He wasn't bitter or angry, Toujou was simply someone he used to know and had since cut ties with, and Amane didn't intend to have anything more to do with him.

"Now that you mention it, you didn't come home for the end-of-year holidays, did you? Your mom must have said something about it."

"I mean, I've got my life in the city, too, and I'm perfectly happy there. Other than checking in with my parents, I don't have any reason to come back here."

"I see."

"So this might be the last time that you and I talk, Hanada."

Just as he had no intention of seeing Toujou again, he wasn't planning to set up a visit with Hanada, either.

With Toujou, it was because Amane had moved on completely. But with Hanada, the circumstances were a little different.

The two of them were no longer friends. In fact, Amane had forgotten Hanada existed until they'd bumped into each other.

"Honestly, I'm probably going to go to college and get a job in the city. If I come back, it'll only be to visit my parents. Even if we reconnect now, our friendship will probably just die out again... I'm not talented enough to maintain a lot of friendships, so rather than keeping up a weak connection that could fade at any time, I'd rather put my efforts into the relationships that really matter to me. Sorry."

It wasn't that Amane hated Hanada, but he knew that he would never feel as strongly about their friendship as he once had. Not to mention the matter of physical distance.

Amane didn't experience a surge of emotion that made him want to continue their relationship. Maybe it was cold of him, but there was a limit to the number of people he could really care about, and he simply didn't have the room to add any more.

Despite the fact that he was being rejected, Hanada simply smiled.

"I'm the one who pulled away from you, so there's no need to apologize," he said. "Even if you wanted to be friends again, I might suspect you had some weird ulterior motive."

Hanada looked down and kicked at a pebble by his feet. After staying silent for a little while, he slowly raised his head.

"In other words, we're good, but we don't need to have anything to do with each other after this, since we live in different places and have different friends. We'll just be former classmates, and that's it. That's what you're saying?"

"That's right," Amane confirmed.

Maybe Amane was being cruel, but Hanada didn't seem hurt.

"I'm actually relieved. I felt guilty about what happened, and it probably would have been impossible for me to forget everything and be best pals like before."

"And I hate the idea of making you worry about me, so I think this is for the best. The other guys probably hardly remember me, and it would feel weird to act all chummy again just because we're from the same town."

"You're exactly right, but…you sure are honest, Amane, coming right out and saying all that when you could've just let things play out."

"Once I saw you, I felt like it wouldn't be right not to say something."

Hanada had been his closest childhood friend before Toujou. After meeting Toujou, Amane had pulled away from him a little. Then, after everything else happened, they'd become quite distant, just two people who happened to interact because they went to the same school.

In a completely different way than with Toujou, Amane felt he ought to say a formal good-bye.

Hanada's eyes darted around a little, then with a smile, he sighed. "…You've really changed, huh? On the outside and the inside."

Amane looked him straight in the eye. "I have, haven't I? Well, I hope I've managed to become a better man."

"I don't know about that, but it seems like you've made a big improvement since I last saw you."

"I guess so; I'm pretty satisfied with how I've been turning out."

Amane was content in a different way than he had been back when he was an innocent child. He felt much happier, and enjoyed himself more than back when he was surrounded by people. That only served to prove how big a role Mahiru played in Amane's life.

"Not gonna lie, I'm pretty jealous. I still haven't got a girlfriend, and I don't stand out in high school."

"I think you can change, if you put in the effort."

"Those words have serious weight, coming from you, Amane."

He was sure Hanada really thought that, now that Amane had left his hometown and had returned looking so different.

Hanada chuckled a bit, then sighed and quietly looked at Amane. "Next time you come back, at least come see Kaname."

"Not you?"

"We just talked about how we were saying good-bye, didn't we? Anyway, how would seeing another guy's face make me happy?"

"Ha-ha, I guess you're right."

"Kaname wasn't disappointed when she saw your girlfriend?"

"Is there anything for her to be disappointed about?"

"She used to have it pretty bad for you, man. She would always go on about how she was going to marry you and stuff."

"I'm not interested in a little girl seven years younger than me."

"Yeah, I know. I guess I just wanted you to understand my pain, as an elder brother who didn't want to crush his baby sister's dreams."

"I suppose you'd be the one in an awkward spot if I became your brother-in-law."

"No kidding."

As Amane cracked a joke, he looked in the direction of the Hanada house, signaling it was probably about time to get going.

Hanada's little sister was smiling and chatting happily with Mahiru, who seemed a little awkward. Suddenly, she looked up, noticed Amane, and silently asked if it was time to go.

Amane nodded calmly.

"Well, I'm keeping my girlfriend waiting, so…"

"All right… Fujimiya."

"Yeah."

Neither of them said "See you later," probably because given what they had just said, they didn't intend to meet again.

Hanada in his hometown and Amane in the city where he lived now—each of them was creating a place where he belonged. And they were both satisfied with that.

Amane had never considered trying to reach out to his former friend. They both understood it wasn't necessary.

It didn't seem like a coldhearted move. They needed to make a clean break.

The fact that Hanada had called him by his surname was just more evidence that things were over between them.

Amane wasn't tactless enough to question it. He just smiled and pretended not to notice, and they quietly parted ways.

Hanada turned his back to Amane and headed toward his house.

Mahiru then trotted over, almost as though she and Hanada were swapping places.

"...Well done," she said.

"It was no big deal." He shrugged. "Did I worry you?"

"Not exactly, I just didn't want you to get hurt."

"If I thought that would happen, I wouldn't have even tried to talk to him... Anyway, I'm fine. I'm glad we got to talk."

"Well then, I'm glad, too."

Amane hadn't planned to meet up with Hanada, but he was glad he had run into him like this. He had been able to clear up some of the uneasiness he still felt about his hometown.

Mahiru saw that Amane wasn't in any distress, and she smiled with relief, her expression relaxed. Amane smiled back and then gently took her hand.

She always seemed to want to hold hands, so he decided to test whether that was true even now. Apparently he was right on the money.

They smiled sheepishly at each other and walked off down the road as the sun began to sink in the sky.

"By the way, Mahiru, Kaname really took a shine to you, didn't she?"

Amane suddenly recalled the scene from a few moments earlier. But when he brought it up, Mahiru avoided meeting his gaze.

"Ah, um, you think…? Mostly, she just badgered me with questions about you, Amane."

"You didn't say anything weird, did you?"

"Of course not. I just talked about how you were getting along well and making friends… It sounds like you were a good big brother to her in the past."

"Are you trying to say that my personality has changed?"

"No, I'm pointing out that you've always been a very caring person."

"…I'm not sure I agree."

"Oh, you might be surprised."

Amane was not as good a person as Mahiru thought, nor as good-natured.

He told her as much, but with a know-it-all look she said, "Like it or not, you're a sweet guy, Amane."

He squeezed Mahiru's hand as if to register his disagreement. Her eyes narrowed, like it tickled. But she didn't revise her appraisal, so Amane kept a sour look plastered on his face and kept fidgeting with Mahiru's hand, trying to make his objections clear.

He knew that her opinion wasn't going to change no matter how long he went on squeezing her hand, so he sighed in defeat and let his fingers intertwine with hers once again. Mahiru blushed as she softly leaned into him.

She was able to get so close because she had closed her parasol. Nearer than before, she looked incredibly radiant, probably because she was bathed in the light of the setting sun.

As they walked slowly along, quietly gazing at the scenery around them, Amane heard a soft, earnest murmur.

"…You've confronted a lot of your past these last few days, haven't you, Amane?"

"I guess I have. First, the main cause of what shaped me into who I am now—and then, someone like a childhood friend I'd grown apart from. In my mind, I left everyone here behind me. I really needed to take another good look at those relationships."

"Surely you don't regret coming home?"

"I think it was, in a very real sense, something I needed to do in order to move forward."

Amane had managed to close the chapter of his life that involved Toujou and also properly dissolve his ties to someone he used to be close with. Amane now understood that both events had been necessary for him to live his new life in the city free of regrets.

"Then it's a good thing we came," said Mahiru.

"All my misgivings are gone, and I feel refreshed. I feel like I can move forward again."

"…You're always looking toward the future, Amane."

"It wouldn't be good to drag things out forever, and now it's clear to me that the past can't weigh me down anymore. I'm glad I came back."

I really have gotten stronger, he thought, taking stock of his own feelings. Though he felt somewhat embarrassed, he pushed the emotion aside. When he looked at Mahiru, he saw that she was silently staring at him.

In fact, that was only how it appeared. The look in her eyes said that she was staring through him, thinking about something else.

"I'm happy to hear that you've gotten past everything, Amane," she murmured.

He could tell that she was being honest, and that was how she truly felt, but he noticed a touch of bitterness mixed in as well.

"…I guess I need to properly face my past, like you have."

Her voice was so quiet that nobody but Amane could hear her, though he wasn't sure if she sensed his confusion.

©Hanekoto

Unable to respond with some lighthearted comment, Amane simply squeezed her hand, which had begun to tremble.

"I can't believe it's really time for you to go!" his mother grumbled, not even trying to hide her sadness. She was standing beside the pillar in front of the ticket gates where they had met at the very start of his homecoming.

His father was there beside his despondent mother, comforting her.

They had already stayed longer than they had initially planned, and of course there was no way they could leave their apartments sitting empty forever, so it was time for Amane to go back to the city—his current home.

Naturally, his mother's reluctant gaze was directed not at him, but at Mahiru. She was clearly upset to part from her darling (intended) daughter-in-law.

"I'm sorry," Mahiru apologized. "But we've got things to do at home—and other plans, so..."

"You don't have to pay attention to anything my mom says. If we start listening to her complaints, we'll be here all day."

"How cold you are. And to your own mother..."

"You're getting what you deserve, Mom, for prioritizing a cute girl over your own son."

"Oh come now, don't act so surprised. Of course I'm going to pay more attention to my adorable, sweet daughter. I don't know when she'll be back, unlike my son, who can visit any time."

She was being utterly shameless, and Amane had already lost any desire to argue with her.

He could kind of understand what she was trying to say, and it seemed like it would be mentally exhausting to continue this any further.

When he glanced over at his father, he caught the man smiling reluctantly, like there was nothing he could do. *Doesn't seem like he'll be any help with Mom.*

Mahiru had looked uneasy, but her delight at his parents' reception must have won out because she was now wearing a wide, embarrassed grin.

"Well, if it's all right with you, I might intrude on you again some…"

"Come anytime! We'll always be ready for you!"

"Let the girl finish her sentence, Mom… But it's a nice offer, isn't it, Mahiru?"

"Yes, it is."

This time, Mahiru's smile was one of pure joy, and when Amane patted her head, his mother looked at them and grinned, though Amane pretended not to see.

"I'm glad that Miss Shiina took a liking to our home," his father added. "Honestly, I was a bit worried about what we would do if she was too reserved."

"I don't think she had much of a chance to be reserved, considering how overbearing Mom was. That probably helped her get acclimated."

"Ha-ha, you're probably right. For better or worse, your mother can be pushy."

"…I don't suppose the two of you are over there speaking ill of me, are you?"

"I think it's one of your charming and desirable traits, my dear."

"Oh, you."

His mother grinned, as if she hadn't been sulking just moments before, and Amane shot her a wry smile in return. Then he looked up at the clock mounted on the wall of the station.

"Well, should we get going?" he asked.

"I guess we should; it's about that time…," said Mahiru.

Amane wanted to hurry up and get settled in their seats, so with some reluctance, they had to part ways.

His parents seemed to understand, and with a regretful look, Amane's mother squeezed Mahiru's hand and pumped it up and down. "Mahiru dear, you come back soon, okay?"

His father looked on with joy in his eyes, then turned again to Mahiru. "Miss Shiina, thank you for coming to visit us. You livened up the place, and it was a lot of fun."

"I—I should be the one thanking you."

"Ha-ha. If you ever fight with Amane, you can tell him 'I'm going home!' and run away to us."

"Do you really think I would hurt Mahiru like that?!"

Amane shot his mother a mean look and got a cheerful smile in return.

"Every couple has a few misunderstandings here and there... Besides, there may be times when you want to be alone or when you want to rely on an adult. So if something happens, you can come here anytime. We will always welcome you."

"...Thanks."

Mahiru's caramel-colored eyes threatened to well up with tears the moment she heard the words *come here anytime*, but the next instant, they were filled with joy.

Amane felt himself tearing up a little, too, as he looked at Mahiru, who looked delighted from the bottom of her heart.

...I wonder if we were able to show Mahiru a little bit of what a happy family looks like?

All he could think about was that, going forward, he wanted to show this girl, who had basically never known a real family, every shade of happiness—and let her experience what it was like.

Mahiru's face relaxed into a soft smile, and Amane grinned peacefully, grasping her hand with affection.

Chapter 6

The Angel and the Suspicious Figure

The first thing Amane did the day after returning to his own apartment was clean.

As expected, he had been too tired to clean the day he got back. Since his place had been empty for a little under two weeks, dust had accumulated. It wasn't that much, but since Mahiru spent time with him in his apartment, he wanted to get it as clean as possible.

To that end, Amane made use of all the cleaning techniques Mahiru had taught him and gave the place a good once-over. Mahiru was apparently busy cleaning her own place, so he did it all by himself.

Though cleaning wasn't exactly Amane's strong suit, thanks to Mahiru's teachings, maintaining a tidy home was no problem.

Mahiru always said, *"If you diligently keep up with your cleaning, you won't need to make any great effort. It's because you put it off that it takes so much unnecessary time and labor."*

Just by doing as she'd taught him and cleaning regularly, he had been able to keep his apartment spick-and-span.

There was only a bit of dust on the furniture, and it was a breeze for Amane to clean up.

He quickly wiped down all the surfaces then did another pass with the vacuum cleaner. While he was at it, he wiped down the windows, too. When that was done, he looked up at the clock.

It was already past three.

His local supermarket usually started marking down their prices at four, so he figured he had better get going.

I've gotten rather accustomed to domestic life, if I do say so myself.

He had cleared out his refrigerator before leaving and had no ingredients for that evening's dinner, so he needed to go shopping. He had gotten by with instant ramen and frozen food for breakfast, but that wouldn't do for dinner.

Amane was responsible for the shopping, but he and Mahiru split the cost of ingredients.

Since they were pooling their money, it seemed only right to buy things as cheaply as possible, but…he wondered if it wasn't a little weird for a high school boy to be worrying about the cost of groceries.

He abruptly laughed at himself and the ways that he had changed. Then he went into his bedroom to put on clean clothes before heading out.

"…Hmm?"

As Amane made his way to the supermarket, lost in thought, a person with a familiar, light hair color passed him by.

He wheeled around to look, but of course all he could see was the person's back.

Their hair was not as long as Mahiru's, and anyway, he could tell that the stranger was a man, so it definitely wasn't her. But his hair didn't look dyed, and it was rare to see such a naturally light color.

Musing on the unusual sight, Amane entered the supermarket. He was tossing ingredients for that evening's dinner into his basket when he heard a familiar voice from behind.

"Oh, fancy meeting you here."

"Kokonoe?"

It was a young man whom Amane had gotten to know through Yuuta, when they had all competed together in the "cavalry battle" at sports day.

Makoto Kokonoe had sweets and juice in his shopping basket, a selection much more typical for a high school boy.

"You live around here, Fujimiya?" he asked.

"Yeah. I didn't think you did, though…"

"I'm just staying over at a friend's house and stopped by to pick up some stuff. And you're here for…dinner?"

"Mm. That's right."

As was plain to see, the basket in Amane's hand was filled with things like raw chicken, daikon radish, milk, and tofu—a world away from snack food.

"That's right, you live alone, don't you? Impressive."

"Well, Mahiru makes all my meals, so it's not all that impressive…"

"…Oh right, you mentioned that before… What an amazing way to live."

"It really is. I'm so grateful to her."

Without Mahiru around, Amane's eating habits would be miserable. Though he had learned to take care of most of the housework thanks to her, he seemed liable to let things slip if left to his own devices.

If she ever went away, there was no chance that Amane would carry on with his current lifestyle.

"I can never repay her," he mumbled with a small, wry smile.

Makoto sighed. "How do I put this, Amane? You're really…you know, head over heels."

"I sure am. And so is Mahiru."

"You say that with such confidence."

"Because I know that she loves me."

He hadn't really believed in her affection before they'd started dating, but things were different now.

He knew that she valued and loved him, and he knew that she wanted to be by his side.

Amane didn't have an inflated ego or anything—he simply registered her feelings as fact. Maybe that was proof he'd become more confident, though it was also true that Mahiru freely directed lots of love his way.

Amane had answered readily and without hesitation, and Makoto was now the one with a wry smile.

"Well, I think it's great that you're so confident about it," he said. "Much better than being all wishy-washy like before, right? Even though it was always clear things were mutual."

"That's harsh."

"I mean, it was so obvious that she was into you. It's none of my business, though, so as long as you guys are happy—everything's good, yeah?"

Makoto shrugged, and Amane smiled, recognizing this as the other boy's way of complimenting him.

"...Plus, Yuuta's given you his blessing, too, so I figure everything worked out peacefully in the end."

"What?"

"Never mind, nothing. Well, I'm going to the register."

Amane was still wondering why Yuuta had come up at all, but Makoto hastily turned and left before Amane could question him about it. Still confused, Amane went back to shopping for the dinner ingredients he had listed on a memo in his phone.

When Amane got back to his apartment building, he spotted the man he had passed on his way to the store looking up at the building.

He had never expected this to be the man's destination, and it was strange that he was still standing outside despite how much time had passed. In spite of himself, Amane stopped in his tracks and watched him.

He had an awfully familiar hair color.

Amane couldn't be sure, since he had only seen the man from behind, but he didn't appear to have a large build. In fact, he was quite slim, and maybe a little bit shorter than Amane.

His head was tilted back as he gazed up at the apartment building.

Though Amane couldn't see his facial expression from where he was standing, there was no question the man was staring intently up at the apartments.

Though Amane was curious about him, he wasn't going to speak to a stranger, so there was nothing to do but slip past. He knew it would be suspicious if he walked by and then suddenly turned around, so he accepted that he probably wouldn't get a good look at the man's face.

Still, unable to give up, Amane double-checked the grocery bags he was carrying, then started walking again.

As he passed the man, Amane let one of the bags bump into him, then dropped it on purpose. He felt a little guilty about the ruse.

The bag only held Amane's snacks and energy bars, so dropping it wouldn't cause any trouble for Mahiru.

When he bumped into the man and dropped the bag, the man's attention shifted to Amane.

As Amane picked up his items and brushed off the dirt, he looked up at the man

He'd expected as much, but a feeling of vindication welled up inside him.

The man was extremely handsome, with clean-cut features that would grab anyone's attention. He was frowning at Amane apologetically, feelings of guilt reflected in his clear, brown eyes.

Since Amane was the one who had intentionally bumped into him, *he* was the one who ought to feel bad about it.

"I'm sorry; that was careless of me," he said.

"No," the man protested. "I'm the one who was standing around in a spot like this; I'm sorry. I was in the way." He apologized in a gentle, low voice that was both composed and calm.

Amane said again, "No, it was my fault," and bowed.

He had confirmed what he'd wanted to confirm. He had no concrete proof, but the man was likely exactly who Amane had thought he was.

Amane went ahead and passed by the man as if nothing had happened.

He probably had no idea who Amane was and didn't have any reason to suspect him.

Though it had only been a ten-second interaction, Amane was feeling strangely worked up, probably because the girl he loved was connected.

He had just made it to the door of the building and breathed a sigh of relief, when—suddenly—that very girl appeared before him.

"Welcome home, Amane."

Amane panicked. He wasn't expecting her to come down to the entry hall—or, in fact, to come greet him at all. Mahiru looked at him in blank puzzlement.

"Why are you making that face?" she asked.

"N-no reason... Just wondering what made you come all the way down here."

"Oh, you sent me a message earlier saying you were coming back soon, didn't you? I asked you to buy a lot of things, so I thought I would help."

"R-right."

It seemed she had genuinely come down to help Amane carry the groceries.

Confirming the man's identity a moment earlier had put a burden on his heart, and now that Mahiru had appeared, it was beating even faster.

Amane worried that its pounding might alert Mahiru to the man's presence, and he turned around to look in spite of himself. But the man who had been there just a moment ago, only about ten meters away, had vanished.

…So he wasn't waiting to see Mahiru, and he wasn't on his way out after meeting her, either.

He could tell it wasn't the latter from the way Mahiru was acting. If the man had come to see her, surely he would have approached after catching sight of her. There would be no reason for him to leave.

So then, *Why,* Amane wondered, *had he come?*

Why had he deliberately walked right up to the front of the apartment building where Mahiru lived, and why had he been staring at the floor she lived on?

"Is something the matter?" asked Mahiru.

"No, it's nothing."

Feeling a little relieved that, for better or worse, Mahiru didn't seem to have noticed the man, Amane placed the bag with the snacks into her waiting hands, then got in the elevator with her.

Later that evening, Amane was looking sidelong at Mahiru, who was sitting beside him, worrying over whether he ought to talk to her about the man he had encountered earlier that day just before she had come down to meet him.

He suspected that the man was Mahiru's father.

Mahiru's mother had an intense, egoistic air about her, and sharp features that hardly resembled Mahiru at all, so it wasn't obvious that they were parent and child. But the man from earlier resembled her so strongly that it was clear at a glance that they were related.

From his gentle, strikingly handsome features, to the color of his hair and eyes, he had looked exactly like Mahiru would if she were a man and a few years older. Naturally, Amane couldn't dismiss him as a stranger, given the resemblance.

He just wasn't sure whether he should say anything to Mahiru.

He knew that she didn't think well of her parents and that she tended to avoid talking about them. If he could, he wanted to act as though nothing had happened.

And yet, if by some chance the man was to show up again and actually approach Mahiru, she was sure to get a shock.

Before that could happen, Amane reasoned, he ought to give Mahiru a chance to prepare herself.

"...Is something on your mind? You've been staring at me for a while."

Amane was fretting over what to do, since either option would be shocking for Mahiru, when she looked at him with a truly puzzled expression. Apparently, she could feel the weight of his gaze.

"Uh, well, how do I put this?"

"What is it—what are you hiding?"

"...I'm not really sure how to tell you."

"If you want to say something, say it. If you don't want to tell me, I won't ask. But if you have something you want to discuss, I'll listen, no matter what it is."

Mahiru was leaving the matter up to Amane. After hesitating for a full ten seconds, he slowly began to speak.

"...So the thing is, earlier...when I went out shopping, I, uh, ran into this man."

"O-oh, did you?"

For the moment, Mahiru just nodded at him. She didn't seem to grasp what he was talking about, so Amane looked her directly in the eyes—ones the same color as those of the man he'd seen earlier.

"He was standing in front of our apartment building, staring up at it...with eyes exactly like yours."

"...Huh?"

Mahiru stiffened, a puzzled expression on her face.

"The man had the same eye and hair color as you, Mahiru. And his face looked like yours, too."

Amane was hinting that the man might be her father, timidly looking for confirmation. To his surprise, Mahiru did not seem shocked, just baffled.

"Hmm... So you're saying that there was a person here who looked like my father?"

"Probably, yeah."

Amane said probably, but in his mind, he was convinced that the man was Mahiru's father. His features and general presence had resembled hers so closely that it seemed absurd to think they could be unrelated.

After blinking several times at Amane's words, Mahiru narrowed her eyes.

She must be in shock, he thought.

"...You're sure it wasn't a case of mistaken identity?" she asked.

"Huh?"

It was Amane's turn to be baffled, this time by her abnormally casual reply.

"My father has never shown any interest in me. For as long as I can remember, I hardly ever saw his face. He's always been completely occupied with work, to the point he must barely remember I exist. Even now, he almost never contacts me, and when he does it's only a business call a couple times a year."

As she told Amane all this in a dispassionate voice, the look in Mahiru's eyes steadily shifted from astonishment to something much colder.

"He has no reason to come and see me, and if he was going to, I'm sure he would send word ahead of time. Though, he's never done anything like that before—not even once," Mahiru asserted decisively.

Amane looked at her face, then squeezed her hand.

"Besides," she continued, "what could he have to say to me at this point? After ignoring his daughter for more than ten years and spending all his time at work, what purpose could my father have for going out of his way to contact me? There's no reason why he would come to see me, at least no reason that I can understand."

"Mahiru."

"Even supposing he did start noticing me now...I can't acknowledge those people as my parents. They are nothing more than two people who happen to be related to me by blood; they are not the parents who raised me. The person who raised me was Miss Koyuki—and nobody else."

Mahiru spoke in a flat, hard voice full of thorns. Her expression was blank, as if she had erased all emotion from her face. Amane found it difficult to look at her, so instead, he embraced her.

The thorns in Mahiru's voice were turned inward, hurting herself more than anyone else.

She didn't seem to be putting on a show of courage. Instead, Amane got the impression that she was mentally wringing her own neck.

He could tell because, even though all the emotion had disappeared from her face, she still seemed to be in pain. She was trying to maintain a blank look, but it seemed obvious to him that she was really hurting.

Wrapped in Amane's arms, Mahiru slowly lifted her head and looked at him.

"...What's this?" she asked.

"...Just missed the warmth of human contact."

"Who did?"

"I did, I guess."

"…Is that so?" Mahiru mumbled quietly, then leaned into Amane and let out a little sigh. "I'm not really worried about it," she said. "He's got nothing to do with me."

"Oh?"

"I've got a new family, after all."

"Mm, I suppose you do."

"…So I'm fine."

"Mm."

Amane was happy that she considered his home to be hers, too. The way she was talking made it clear how she felt about her own. Sensing this, he gently stroked her head.

"…So then, if I happen to catch sight of that person again, what should I do?" he asked, gently running his hand over her hair.

Mahiru was leaning against Amane's chest, so when he asked his question, she slowly looked up and stared at him with calm eyes. There was no shock or anguish in her expression, which came as a relief.

Then Mahiru frowned, looking a little uncomfortable under his gaze.

"…I don't care; you can do whatever you like," she said.

"You don't want me to do anything in particular?"

He had been certain that she would ask him not to approach the man, but Mahiru only shook her head.

"Not really… Not unless we run into him together, or if he tries to speak to me while I'm alone or something. If you encounter him on your own, Amane, I'm not going to tell you how to react. I'd still like you to report to me that you saw him, though."

"…I see. So you're planning to not get involved with him in any way—is that what I'm hearing?"

"Yes… If he's got something he wants to say to me, he can make an appointment and say it directly—or contact me by email. Lurking around watching me is just plain weird. If he's not going to reach out himself, I'm not going to do anything. So long as he doesn't do anything to threaten my lifestyle, I'm going to ignore him."

Mahiru did seem curious about the presence of a man who resembled her father, but she didn't want to go out of her way to make contact with him.

In Mahiru's position, Amane might have done the same. But the way she made up her mind to ignore someone who was basically confirmed to be her father once again made it clear to Amane how deeply she resented her parents.

Mahiru nuzzled back into Amane's chest sweetly, and he simply responded, "Gotcha." Then he wrapped his arms under her knees and around her back, scooped her up, and set her down sideways in his lap.

He chuckled slightly at Mahiru's startled expression, then pressed his lips to her forehead to comfort her. She immediately flushed bright red and buried her face in his chest once again.

This time, she must have been doing it to hide her embarrassment because she was smacking her forehead into him, head-butting him with considerable force. That, too, was charming, and Amane smiled in spite of himself.

"…Well, I'm not you, and I can't really interfere in another person's family matters, but…I think it's best for you to do as you see fit, and I'll support you in whatever you decide."

Amane was, after all, an outsider. Though, of course, he'd like to think that was only temporary.

He wouldn't get involved in Mahiru's family issues. As long as that was what she wanted, he would merely support her quietly from the sidelines.

He was determined to stay by her side, no matter what her family situation was.

If she said she wanted to run away from home, he was prepared to help make that happen.

Mahiru acknowledged Amane's words with a quiet "Okay."

He ruffled her hair and said, "Don't worry, if push comes to shove, I'll sweep you away." He spoke in a teasing whisper, just barely loud enough for Mahiru to hear.

She lifted her head suddenly with great force and looked at him, her face flushed red, so Amane feigned innocence and stroked Mahiru's hair some more.

Several days had passed since Amane had encountered the man he suspected was Mahiru's father.

For the time being, Amane was on alert, looking out for him whenever he left the house. But contrary to his fears, he hadn't seen hide nor hair of him.

It was only a guess, but Amane imagined that Mahiru's father had come to meet with her, or to see how she was doing, only to end up hesitating when it came time to actually approach her. Otherwise, he would have spoken to her by now.

Amane had asked Mahiru about it, and according to her, her father hadn't made contact or shown up again. He probably didn't intend to see her, at least not for now.

"...I really don't get it..."

He figured Mahiru's father had come to see her, but his motives remained unclear, leaving Amane with a lingering sense of unease.

That said, he didn't intend to involve himself too deeply, so as long as the man didn't make contact, Amane wouldn't take any action, either.

"What's the matter?"

"I'm just worried about something," he replied.

Amane had been staring at Itsuki's summer homework as he grumbled to himself. Now Itsuki was looking at him with a curious expression.

"It's rare for you to be worried enough to say something, Amane," he said. "Come on, tell your big brother all about it."

"What are you talking about? You're younger than me."

"Don't sweat the small stuff. Now, out with it."

Apparently, Itsuki had lost interest in his studies.

He had tossed his mechanical pencil down on the desk, turned to face Amane, and was patting his own chest, as if to say *Leave it to me.*

…*What should I do?*

Of course, there was no way that Amane could tell Itsuki about Mahiru's family situation.

No matter how close of a friend Itsuki might be, it wasn't Amane's place to reveal something that Mahiru had decided to keep a secret.

If it had been about Amane, he probably would have confided in his friend, but ultimately, this was Mahiru's business and not his. There was no way he could talk about it openly.

But at the same time, he would never reach an answer by worrying over it alone.

After keeping quiet for a little while, Amane spoke up, choosing his words carefully. "If someone who had refused to have anything to do with you up until now suddenly tried to make contact, what would you think was going through their head?"

"Is this about you?"

"No comment."

"Hmm. Fine, it doesn't really matter."

The look in Itsuki's eyes implied he had an inkling of what Amane was talking about, but he didn't probe any deeper and simply accepted his friend's words at face value. Then his expression turned pensive.

"Well, it depends on the situation, but…they didn't get in touch first?"

"Nope."

"Hmm. And this person, they're not a stalker, are they?"

"…I think they've stopped just shy of stalking."

The man had stealthily come to their apartment building and then vanished without so much as a peep the moment Mahiru appeared. He couldn't quite be called a stalker, but he was definitely suspicious.

"That 'just shy' worries me, but…from what you've said, you sound right to be concerned about them. I don't know what your relationship with them is like, but maybe they've got important business that needs to be discussed in person, or maybe they've had a change of heart that made them want to reach out—or something."

"…A change of heart?"

"If they're making the effort to get in contact now, despite being the one who refused it previously, then that's the only explanation, isn't it?" Itsuki shrugged, reiterating that he didn't know all the details.

Amane forced a smile. "You may be right."

If what Itsuki was saying was true, it made sense for Mahiru's father to visit her. However, his reasons still weren't clear.

Amane didn't know anything about Mahiru's father's personality or circumstances, so even if he wanted to try to imagine the man's thought process, he didn't have a single clue to guide him.

The best he could come up with was that something might have happened that affected his circumstances or state of mind. That was the only reason he could imagine for the man to come see Mahiru now.

"Like I said, I can't really talk because I don't know all the details, but if it were me, I think I'd get curious and end up contacting them. I hate letting things sit like that. I get too antsy."

"That sounds just like you…"

"But you're more of a passive guy, Amane, so why don't you just wait until the other person makes contact? I bet they'll reach out again before too long, if that's really what's going on. And if they give up, there's always email or a phone call."

When Itsuki pointed out that, without knowing the other party's situation, waiting was the only option, Amane reached the same conclusion. After all, he had no way of solving the problem as things were now.

Mahiru was the one at the heart of all this, so there was nothing he could do.

Amane sighed, resigning himself, and Itsuki's lips turned up in amusement.

"...Well, do your best for your beloved, young man."

"Wha—?"

"You're surprisingly easy to read, you know. If this was about you, you would have just come out and said it. You only get this worked up when it has to do with Miss Shiina."

"...Can it, will you?"

"I don't have the right to meddle too much in other people's affairs, so I'll just leave it at this, but I think you should do everything you can for your sweet girlfriend, you hear?"

Itsuki poked Amane with his elbow, and Amane's face twisted into a sullen grimace.

"I know, I know. Geez," he answered quietly.

Chapter 7

A Summer Festival with the Angel

"Did you know that today is the summer festival?"

Chitose had suddenly come over to Amane's apartment one afternoon a week before the end of summer break, only to eventually pose that question.

"...I did, but—"

"Oh, maybe you have plans to go with Mahiru? I already invited Itsuki."

"We didn't exactly make plans, but I was going to ask her."

He knew that Mahiru didn't have anything else to do that day, so he had been thinking of taking her to the festival as a surprise.

He'd gone ahead and asked his mother to send him some *yukata* so the two of them could go out together.

"Huh?" Mahiru, who was returning from pouring them some tea, looked at Amane with a blank expression.

"You wanted to go to a summer festival, so I looked into it," he said.

Mahiru blinked repeatedly.

"...Am I butting in where I don't belong?" asked Chitose.

"No. I'd be fine going alone with Mahiru, but if you two are already going, maybe we should spend the time all together while we still can."

Amane and his friends were already in their second year of high school, and after summer break, their classes would be even more focused on college entrance exams.

Their school's program was designed so that the students finished all the course content that was normally learned over three years in just two, then the remaining year was spent focused on their future courses of study, covering what each student needed to learn to prepare for their higher education. That meant their classes would be fairly fast-paced.

In other words, they wouldn't have much free time to goof off or relax without thinking about school. Once they advanced to their third year, they would not only be studying at home, but attending prep school, cram school, and lessons with private tutors. Chances to spend time with friends would become incredibly rare.

It would be easy for Amane to find time to spend alone with Mahiru, but it was going to get really hard to line up everyone's schedules all at once.

"...What do you think, Mahiru?"

"I'd be delighted if we could go with everyone. Though, I would like it if you let me know ahead of time before you show up for a visit, Chitose."

"I said sorry. And I did try."

"Ten minutes before you arrived..."

After handing a glass of chilled barley tea to Chitose, Mahiru smiled wryly as she sneakily exposed what her friend had done.

Amane recalled how baffled Mahiru had been when she told him that Chitose was on her way. That was why he had put off asking

Mahiru to the summer festival and turned his attention to the sudden, perplexing visit.

Itsuki had surprised him by turning up at his apartment before, but he'd never expected Chitose to do the same.

She had probably come over because she was confident they were at home, but still, he would have liked her to tell them a little earlier.

He let out a sigh as he watched Chitose happily suck down her ice-cold barley tea, then glanced over at Mahiru.

She didn't seem particularly opposed to going to the festival.

Amane had thought she seemed a little down, perhaps due to the recent issues with her father, so he wanted to take her out for a diversion. Her father might still try to get in contact with her, but maybe Amane could make her forget about him for a little while.

"Sounds like everything's settled, then," said Chitose. "So how about it, Mahiru? You gonna wear a *yukata*?"

"Huh? Oh, unfortunately I don't have any."

"Actually, um… I have one here. In your size," Amane cut in.

"Why would *you* have one?"

"I asked my mom to send it over."

As soon as he brought up his mother, Mahiru made a noise of understanding. Perhaps she'd assumed his mother simply had a lot of clothing in her size. Amane couldn't laugh, however, because her assumption wasn't too far off the mark.

Amane didn't complain this time, since he was the one who had made the request, but it did make him wonder why his mother had so much clothing for young women lying around. It was true that she worked in fashion, but she had obviously purchased the clothes specifically for Mahiru.

"Mahiru's going to wear a *yukata*?" Chitose cried excitedly. "I wanna see!"

"Oh, but aren't you wearing one, too?"

"No way. *Yukata* are cute, but they're hard to move in, and with the obi and everything, it doesn't seem like I'd be able to eat as much as I want."

"You sure that's not just because you eat like a pig, Chitose?"

"Rude!"

Chitose didn't like tight clothing, plus she was the type to eat well and move around a lot, so it seemed like *yukata* and other clothing that demanded a certain gracefulness from the wearer were not really her style.

It wasn't easy for anyone to move in *yukata*, so it would undoubtedly be uncomfortable for an active person like Chitose.

"Oh yeah, so what's Itsuki gonna do?"

"He's planning to meet us there."

"You decided that before you even invited us? I'm getting the feeling you assumed we were going from the get-go…"

"Heh-heh, I figured you two wouldn't turn me down, so long as you were free."

"You really ought to give more thought to other people's plans."

"Sorry, sorry!"

Amane glared at Chitose, who didn't seem sorry at all, but there was nothing more to be done.

Amane had told Itsuki in a text message that they had no plans for the next several days, and he figured that was why Itsuki and Chitose had come up with the idea to invite them.

He still wished that Chitose had given them a heads up, but this would be a nice change of pace, so he was grateful for the invitation.

"So then, Mahiru, what do you want to do?" he asked. "Do you want to wear a *yukata*?"

"…Won't I stand out, if I'm the only one wearing one?"

"Actually, I was planning to wear one, too…"

"Huh, you have one?"

"I thought I might wear one, to make the occasion more memorable."

"Amane in a *yukata*..."

Mahiru suddenly started fidgeting, and a little voice inside Amane grumbled that he didn't think it was all that interesting to see a man wearing a *yukata*.

He wasn't necessarily putting himself down, but women's *yukata* had a showiness to them that men's *yukata* usually did not. Wearing one would put him in the right mood for a festival, but he didn't think it was anything worth getting excited over.

But Mahiru was shooting glances at him, as if to say she wanted to see it. If that was what his adorable girlfriend wanted, then he intended to grant her wish. Since he'd be next to Mahiru, he figured he might as well look his best.

"Well, if that's what you want, Mahiru, then I'll gladly wear one."

"I—I want to see."

"That was quick. I don't mind, but don't get your hopes up. Mine is just an ordinary *yukata*."

Amane's outfit had a simple, conservative color combination—a plain navy blue *yukata* and a reddish-brown obi belt, so it wouldn't stand out or catch anyone's attention.

And yet Mahiru was looking at him with eyes full of expectation, so he forced a smile and said, "All right, I'll try to wear it well," patting her head.

An hour and a half before the festival began, Amane and Mahiru started to get ready.

Accompanied by Chitose, Mahiru took her *yukata* back to her own apartment, and Amane shifted his focus to dressing himself.

It required some know-how to put on even a simple *yukata*, but he wasn't concerned about Mahiru. She knew her way around a kimono, so surely she could easily put on something like a *yukata*.

Amane was the problem, and even though his mother had drilled the process into him, he had never actually put on a *yukata* by himself before, so he was anxious about whether he could do it well.

After he finished getting ready, Amane checked himself over in the mirror. Everything looked correct, and nothing appeared sloppy or out of place.

His *yukata* was basic, a plain navy blue with a reddish-brown obi. Amane didn't like intense, overly bold patterns, so he was grateful for its simplicity.

His reflection more or less looked the part, aided by the fact that he was on the taller side.

For better or worse, Amane had always had gentle features, so he naturally looked calm and collected, and the outfit looked good on him.

Whether he looked all right next to Mahiru was something he would leave up to other people's judgment.

He was anxious about the scrutiny he would get from those around him, but in the end, what mattered was what he thought—and what Mahiru thought.

Amane was the first to finish changing and doing his hair, so he sat on the sofa to relax as he waited.

He knew that it took girls a long time to dress up. They had plenty of time to spare, so it was no problem whatsoever.

He figured putting on a *yukata* would be even more involved, and since girls usually wore their hair up with such outfits, styling it would no doubt take somewhere in the realm of three times longer.

On top of all that, she would also probably put on makeup.

Girls are amazing, thought Amane with genuine awe. *Of course,*

Mahiru is cute without doing a thing, but when girls get dressed up, they sparkle even more. Incredible.

Amane found Mahiru's efforts to look cute for her boyfriend touching, and he felt unspeakably blessed.

As he was leisurely waiting on the couch, he heard the sound of his front door unlocking and realized that she must have been finished getting ready.

He was looking forward to seeing her all dressed up, but he didn't turn to look. Instead, he waited for her to approach.

"Amane." She called his name quietly and tapped his shoulder.

That was when he finally turned around—and smiled.

"You're so cute. It looks amazing on you."

"…Y-you can't possibly judge that so quickly."

"I can too. All I needed was one look."

Mahiru seemed a little suspicious, like she thought he had prepared his words ahead of time, but that was his honest reaction, so there was nothing else he could say.

Once again, he was keenly aware of how good his mother was at choosing clothes.

She must have taken into consideration that Mahiru would be standing by his side because Mahiru's *yukata*, adorned with hydrangeas on a white background, gave off a bright impression while still maintaining a subdued, elegant air.

The flowers were painted in dark blues and purples, giving them depth and producing a mature, polished feeling. Hydrangeas were usually worn a little earlier in the year, but they suited Mahiru extremely well.

Her obi was a brighter shade of purple, a lovely color that set off the simple design of her *yukata*, and her *obidome* cord was embellished with a glass bead, giving it a fresh feeling.

Amane gazed steadily at Mahiru's figure. She was the very embodiment of elegance. He smiled.

"You're always cute, but today you look extra polished and grown-up. I guess you could say you look sexy, in a graceful way. I said you were cute, and I meant it, but more than that, you look beautiful. Yeah, it's perfect on you."

"O-oh, okay."

His honest impression seemed to have embarrassed Mahiru, and she played with a strand of hair at the side of her face. Seeing this brought another smile to his face.

Mahiru had done up her hair, securing it with a *kanzashi* ornament. Whenever she moved, little silver chains on the hairpin swayed along with her motion.

The *kanzashi* was decorated with a combination of navy blue natural stone and glass beads in a design similar to the one on her obi. In a way, it gave off a similar feeling to Amane's *yukata*.

"Mahiru, Mahiru, he really means it!" Chitose exclaimed.

"I know that; I'm just letting it sink in."

"...Are you criticizing me, by any chance?" Amane asked.

"Praising but criticizing at the same time, maybe?" replied Chitose.

"What does that mean?"

Amane narrowed his eyes, unsure of Chitose's intention, but the girl only laughed, and Mahiru fidgeted and drew in on herself bashfully, so he couldn't press her for an answer, either.

Mahiru seemed pretty pleased, however, so he figured it couldn't be that bad.

"...A-Amane," said Mahiru. "You look really good, too."

"You think so? Thanks. It makes me really happy to hear that from you."

He had thought that the ensemble was more or less flattering, but it was a big deal to get confirmation from Mahiru. He got the feeling that his girlfriend was a little biased in his favor, but the compliments were still nice.

He thought everything was going okay, but for some reason, Mahiru's expression turned a little peevish.

"...Did I do something wrong?" he asked.

"I think she's mad 'cause it's not fair she's the only one blushing."

"Ch-Chitose!"

Mahiru's flustered reaction only served to prove Chitose right.

Apparently Mahiru wanted to make Amane blush, too, but this wasn't enough to get him flustered. He was happy, and a bit self-conscious, but not as much as Mahiru was.

Chitose smiled happily as she clung to Mahiru, who was clearly shaken, and cooed, "You sweet thing!"

Her ability to touch Mahiru without messing up the other girl's hair, clothes, or makeup was genuinely impressive. Amane, however, wasn't sure whether he should be in awe or assert that he was the only one allowed to fawn over her like that.

But when he saw Mahiru blush, he quickly forgave Chitose. Mahiru was so cute that he didn't mind watching the two of them play around, so he decided to simply stand by and keep an eye on them.

"Whoa, *yukata*!"

They got off at the train station closest to the festival grounds, where Itsuki was already waiting.

It seemed he hadn't expected them to wear *yukata*, and his eyes went wide in admiration when he saw Amane's and Mahiru's outfits.

"Hey, Itsuki, it's been a few days. My mom sent over both of these."

"Wow, her judgment is terrific. They look great on you."

"My mother has a ridiculously good sense for things like this."

He and Mahiru looked like two peas in a pod. Their *yukata* were well matched, as if chosen to go side by side. In spite of himself, Amane was impressed.

He resolved to send his mother a photo of Mahiru in her *yukata* later along with his thanks, then turned back to Itsuki.

The other boy usually dressed casually, but today he had put on a decent pair of jeans and a nice shirt and looked great. Being that handsome had to be a sin.

Amane had no doubt that a *yukata* would have suited his friend well. But he knew that Itsuki didn't really want to wear one, so he held his tongue.

"Oh yeah," Itsuki said. "It's a sight for sore eyes to see a pretty girl in a *yukata*!"

"Wait a second, Itsuki, what about me—?"

"Oh, Chi. You're cute no matter where you go or what you do."

"...How can you say that, after doubling over laughing when I put on a face mask?"

"You looked cute like that, too, I swear!"

"You're laughing just thinking about it, aren't you?!"

Itsuki's shoulders were shaking with mirth even as Chitose smacked him. Mahiru shot him a wry grin, as well.

Amane had seen Mahiru with a beauty mask stuck to her face when they were home visiting his parents, but rather than thinking it was weird or funny, he remembered being impressed at how hard it was to maintain her looks—and by how admirable she was for putting in the work.

At the time, Amane had nearly fallen victim to the face mask himself, though he ultimately turned it down.

Recognizing that she had also worked hard on her beautiful

makeup, Amane stroked Mahiru's cheek gently with the back of his finger so he wouldn't smear any, and Mahiru laughed ticklishly.

That was enough to make the people around them watching gasp, reminding Amane once again what a beautiful girl he was dating.

"I guess when your girlfriend is that cute, she really stands out, huh?" he remarked.

"Actually, I think it's the two of you standing side by side that's drawing all the attention…," said Itsuki.

"Well, I guess that's inevitable, since hardly anyone wears a *yukata* to summer festivals these days."

"You may be right, but I think it's a little more than just that… Well, whatever." Itsuki shrugged in exasperation.

Amane ignored him and gently pulled Mahiru toward him, hoping to ward off attention from others and make it clear she was his. Mahiru blinked a few times, but she must have understood the meaning behind his actions because she blushed slightly and cheerfully clung to Amane's arm.

Both Chitose and Itsuki grinned, but Mahiru didn't seem to mind as she cuddled up to Amane.

"We're not going to let them outdo us, are we?" said Chitose.

"Ha-ha-ha, get over here," Itsuki said in reply.

Amane smiled in resignation at his two friends as they excitedly drew closer to each other, unwilling to lose. Then he looked down at Mahiru, who was clinging tightly to him.

Her eyes were filled with trust as she looked up at him, so Amane responded by squeezing her small hand.

"Should we get going, then?" he said. "We won't get anywhere standing around."

"The festival's already started," Chitose pointed out, before exclaiming, "Whoo-hoo, let's eat!"

She clung to Itsuki's arm and raised her other hand excitedly, though she sounded more interested in the food than in him. Itsuki smiled at her, then they turned toward the festival grounds and started walking.

Amane looked Mahiru in the eye and smiled, then grasped her hand tightly and followed after the others.

By the time the four friends arrived, the festival grounds were already bustling with activity.

The event was being held in an area that normally had little pedestrian traffic, but on that day, it was overflowing with people.

There hadn't been any other festivals nearby for the past two or three weeks, which probably contributed to this one's success.

At first glance, there were very few people dressed in *yukata*, so it seemed like he and Mahiru would really stand out, though Mahiru's beauty was also a big factor.

"There are so many people here!" said Chitose.

"There sure are," Itsuki replied. "We've gotta be careful not to lose sight of one another."

"Mahiru, you can't let go of Amane, no matter what, okay?"

"...I won't," she said.

As Mahiru snuggled up close to Amane, she gripped his hand even tighter, and in response, Amane squeezed hers back, entwining their fingers and vowing never to let her go.

He was sure that if he wasn't holding her hand, rude guys would swarm her, waiting to make a pass. They'd never be able to resist a girl as cute as Mahiru.

Itsuki whistled at the two of them, and Amane shot him a look, pointing out that he was holding hands with his girlfriend, too. Then he gazed out over the stall-lined street ahead.

"Mahiru, is there anything you want to see? Or something you want to eat?"

"It's my first time at an event like this, so I don't really know what's here…"

"Oh, right. Well, a safe first choice is to eat something, I guess."

Remembering that Mahiru's family had hardly ever taken her out put Amane in a gloomy mood, but he smiled to encourage her, and she smiled a little, too.

"Ah, I wanna get cotton candy!" Chitose said.

"If we buy that at the beginning, it'll be a pain to carry around, and if you don't finish it, it'll get all soggy…"

Chitose had a big appetite, and if she finished it off right away, it wouldn't be a problem. But Amane couldn't help feeling it was better to have proper food before dessert.

Amane would have been perfectly happy to chow down on some *yakisoba* or *takoyaki*, but he was worried about the sauce getting on his *yukata*, and above all, he wanted to prioritize what Mahiru wanted.

"…What kind of things do they have at festivals?" she asked.

"For dinner, there's things like *yakisoba* and *takoyaki*, as well as grilled squid, hot dogs, and so on. There's lots of things to fill you up, if that's what you're looking for."

"…Would it be all right to decide as we walk around?"

"That's fine with me. That's what festivals are all about, after all."

While it was fine to head right for what you wanted, there was something nice about wandering around and buying whatever looked good. In fact, that was probably the best way to enjoy a festival.

Amane shot a questioning look toward Itsuki and Chitose, who both nodded in agreement. With their approval, he chose a direction, and urging Mahiru along, he walked off into the crowd.

As they strolled aimlessly down the street, taking in all the stalls and buying things to eat, a shooting gallery—a festival favorite— came into view.

Amane thought of shooting galleries as particularly festive

attractions, and since this was a rare opportunity, he really wanted to take a turn. Though, if Mahiru didn't show any interest, he was prepared to skip it.

She was still holding his hand, looking excitedly around at all the stalls, her eyes sparkling with delight. She followed Amane's line of sight and blinked several times.

"Amane, what's that?"

"Oh, that's a shooting gallery. It's a game where you take aim at a prize with a cork gun, and if you knock it down, you get to keep it. Want to try?"

Thinking that everything could be an experience, he pulled out his wallet and shook it back and forth. Mahiru looked a little perplexed, but her curiosity must have gotten the better of her because she gave a little nod.

Amane excitedly handed his money over to the stallkeeper, accepted a gun and five cork bullets, and loaded it up so Mahiru could shoot. He was able to do it all himself without the stallkeeper's help because his parents had taken him to countless festivals.

"Here, all set. What do you want to aim for?"

"...I think those are cute."

The prize Mahiru pointed out was a set of hairpins in a plastic case. The pins, which were decorated with hydrangeas, would match the *yukata* she was wearing, and they had a charming design.

But drawing from his own experience, Amane knew that those types of prizes were often set up to be quite difficult to drop, so he wouldn't usually recommend that a first-timer aim for one.

That said, he wanted to respect Mahiru's decision, so he didn't say anything. He left it all in Mahiru's hands, simply instructing her on her stance and how to shoot.

He watched, privately enjoying the sight of a beautiful girl readying a gun, even if it was basically a toy. With a truly serious expression, Mahiru leveled the barrel and pulled the trigger.

There was a soft pop, and the cork bullet went flying...straight into the fabric behind the prizes.

"Grr, this is hard!" she said.

"To be honest, even aiming is going to be pretty hard on your first go."

It was a mistake to underestimate the difficulty just because there wasn't that much distance between the shooter and the prize.

Depending on the force and muzzle velocity of the gun, the angle would need to be adjusted, and a shooter also had to make sure not to shift when they fired. Each gun also had its own quirks, and without first ascertaining those, it was sometimes impossible to even graze a prize.

Amane laughed at himself for putting so much thought into it, recalling the techniques and knowledge his parents had drilled into him. Mahiru must have misunderstood, however, and thought he was laughing at her.

"This time, for sure, I'm going to hit it," she said enthusiastically, before inserting the cork bullet the way Amane had shown her and firing.

But ultimately, she missed every shot, and all of that energy turned into sighs of disappointment.

The stallkeeper handed her several corn puff snacks as a consolation prize, and Mahiru looked dejected.

"I lost," she said.

"It was your first time, so I'm not surprised," Amane pointed out.

"Right? Everyone misses their first shot!" Chitose added. "Amane'll get revenge for you. Come on, Amane, I wanna see you look cool!"

"Don't butt in and make promises for other people," Amane shot back.

Amane had been planning to take on the challenge if Mahiru wasn't successful, but now that Chitose had said it so casually, he'd be in trouble if he couldn't win the prize.

Still, Mahiru seemed pretty sad about her failure. She looked at the hairpins she had been aiming for, then up at Amane.

"...I want them," she said, giving him an adorable pleading look. Chitose had definitely taught her that one.

"...Well, if you say that, I've got to try my best, don't I?" Amane said with a strained smile. "Can't afford to lose now." He handed his fee over to the stallkeeper and took the gun and cork bullets.

It had been a while, and he wasn't sure how well he'd do. He checked the feeling of the gun and tried not to get too worked up as he assumed his stance and pulled the trigger.

With a smooth motion, the cork bullet flew straight for the hairpin case, just grazing the edge of it.

Although the case did sway a bit, it didn't fall.

"You were so close!" Chitose said.

"No, that was good. That shot was just to get a feel for it and to see what quirks the gun itself has."

He'd never thought he could take it down in one shot. That was only a test run, and yet he had actually managed to graze the prize.

From the feel of the gun and how it had fired, and judging by how close he had come to hitting the prize, he got the sense that with the guns at this stall, he could probably do it.

Depending on the quality of the gun, sometimes a shot was impossible, so he was glad that this one seemed to pose no problem. As long as his aim was good, and he hit the right spot, he figured he could knock down most of the prizes.

Feeling relieved that he hadn't lost his touch, Amane loaded the gun a second time and aimed.

If it was for Mahiru, he would do his best to hit anything, even the huge stuffed animal that was the grand prize. But she wanted those hairpins, so that was where he aimed.

This takes me back.

He had often gone to festivals when he was in elementary and middle school. As those memories floated up in his mind, he calmly pulled the trigger, and this time, he hit the case slightly above center.

He hadn't been sure whether he could drop the prize by hitting it dead center, so he had carefully aimed his shot to knock it wildly off balance, focusing on taking advantage of its center of gravity. Just as he'd planned, the case swung wide and then fell.

A faint commotion could be heard from the other customers around him. Apparently, he had an audience.

If he'd missed with so many people watching, he would have been pretty embarrassed. Amane half-heartedly shot his remaining bullets at some sweets that looked easy to knock over, scoring a few more prizes. The stallkeeper's cheerful smile had a bit of a twitch to it.

I guess it's bad for his business if I win too much, huh?

Recalling the time that his mother had almost gotten banned for winning too many prizes in one go, Amane apologized with a shrug and accepted his hard-won loot.

"This is what you wanted, right?"

When he turned around and offered Mahiru the case of hairpins, she nodded bashfully.

"…Th-thank you so much. I never thought they would actually fall…"

"Yeah, how'd you get those so easily?" Chitose demanded.

"Guess I'm just good at this kind of thing."

"Wow, what a hunk. How aggravating."

"What the heck…?"

Chitose had been the one egging him on, but now that he had actually won the prize, she was complaining. Amane found it absurd.

"You know, Amane is pretty good at this kind of thing," Itsuki remarked. "He always gets high scores in the shooting games at arcades and stuff, too."

"My parents put a lot of effort into teaching me useless skills like this… They said it would enrich my life…"

"And thanks to that, you were able to get the prize that Miss Shiina wanted, so it's all good, right?"

"I guess so."

It was true that he had been able to win the prize Mahiru wanted, so he was grateful to his parents. At this rate, he could probably claim cork gun–shooting as a special talent.

With a smile, Amane took one of the prize hairpins out of its case, gently held a lock of Mahiru's bangs between his fingers, and fixed the pin in place.

Purely by chance, the design of the hairpin resembled the print on her *yukata*, and they went together well. It matched her whole look.

"Mm, cute. That looks great on you."

It suited her, and when he peered down at Mahiru's face, he noted that, though simple, the pin had a cute design and seemed easy to use.

"Thank you," she whispered, her cheeks a rosy pink.

"Amane, you're such a flirt, but only with Miss Shiina," noted Itsuki, just as Amane noticed Mahiru's blush.

Amane ignored Itsuki's nonsensical comment and stroked his girlfriend's head. She looked both embarrassed and delighted.

"Mahiru's certainly in a good mood," Chitose remarked.

Wearing the hairpin that Amane had gotten for her, Mahiru looked extremely cheerful.

©Hanekoto

She was so radiant that Chitose felt compelled to point it out.

Not only that, the glow of her sweet smile could be felt all around her, and if she wasn't careful, Cupid might start launching arrows straight into the hearts of any men who saw her—a frightful prospect.

Though this captivating beauty was the very picture of an angel, her smiling face had something of a devilish quality to it.

This was the first time Itsuki had seen Mahiru in such high spirits, and even he shrank back shyly.

Amane, too, who ought to have developed a certain degree of resistance, couldn't control the throbbing in his chest.

"Hey, Amane, you've got to put a stop to this," Itsuki said.

"I know. She's adorable, but I feel sorry for her victims."

He wouldn't want anything to happen to the happily smiling Mahiru, either. So Amane gently tugged at her hand and brought his mouth to her ear.

"Mahiru. I'm glad you're so happy, but you can't show that kind of face to other people. A bad guy might come and abduct you…and besides—"

"Besides, what?"

"…I guess I just wish that you'd save such a cute face for when the two of us are alone together. I want you to reserve it just for me."

He whispered in a voice only Mahiru could hear, asking her not to show that face to anyone else, which made her turn such an intense shade of red that he thought he could hear her ignite.

Mahiru nodded firmly. She looked eager, courageous, and adorable, but the hairpin from a moment earlier began slipping.

Holding her still, Amane gently fixed the placement of the pin. While he was at it, he stroked her cheek, and this time Mahiru froze before softly butting her forehead against his upper arm, hiding her face.

Realizing that she was probably embarrassed, Amane stroked her hand in his with the pad of his thumb. That got a reaction out of her, so she couldn't be completely overwhelmed.

"Hey, you two, it's all very well that the onslaught has stopped, but this is hard to watch," Itsuki interjected.

"Mahiru's so cute that I can't help it," Amane replied.

"Actually, I think it's all your fault this time... I wish those girls who pegged you as gloomy could see what a stud you are now."

"Where's this coming from all of a sudden?"

"Mahiru's got a weakness for Amane, too," Chitose added. "His destructive power grows and grows!"

Amane looked down at Mahiru, who was still clinging to him, as he wondered with exasperation what Itsuki meant by calling him a stud. For some reason, his girlfriend was glaring up at him.

"...Amane," she said. "What you said earlier, right back at you."

"O-oh?"

"I mean it."

She nodded, emphasizing her point. Then, looking a little relieved, Mahiru ground her forehead into his upper arm.

He let her do as she pleased, musing that she seemed to really like head-butting him, then saw Chitose grinning at them.

"As usual, you've got a natural seductiveness that only works on Mahiru," she said.

"Seductiveness... Look here—"

"Now, I won't stand in your way, since sweet Mahiru seems to like it, but...more importantly, I'm hungry, so why don't we go buy some of that grilled squid over there? After all that sweet stuff, I feel like eating something salty."

"You haven't had anything sweet to eat yet, have you...?"

"I'm not talking about food; I'm talking about you two. Anyway, let's go, for the sake of our peanut gallery."

At that, Amane glanced around them, and his eyes landed on a number of people blushing.

Men and women both seemed to be affected by Mahiru's adorable behavior. He was getting looks of simple jealousy from the men, so there could be no doubt.

Realizing he shouldn't have embarrassed Mahiru in such a public place, Amane decided to go along with Chitose's suggestion and started walking toward the grilled squid stall, pulling Mahiru along by the hand.

"Mmm, food just tastes different at a festival, doesn't it? It must be the atmosphere."

Even though she had already eaten *yakisoba* noodles and fried chicken, Chitose was chowing down on some grilled squid like she had room to spare. She looked truly delighted.

They were standing and eating in a rest area that had been set up a short distance away from the food stalls lining the main thoroughfare. But even there, Amane could feel people looking at them as he glanced around.

Well, Mahiru and Chitose may be different types, but they're both beautiful.

Mahiru was the embodiment of polished, sweet beauty, and Chitose was lively and winsome, with a boyish appeal. They each had their own style, but the fact that they were both beautiful young ladies was undeniable.

Of course they attracted attention.

And that wasn't all—at the moment, Chitose was feeding Mahiru a bite of her grilled squid, since Mahiru had been staring at it hungrily. The men in the crowd couldn't take their eyes off the two lovely girls acting so friendly with each other.

Amane could hear men letting out spellbound sighs as Mahiru

Saekisan * 157

smiled softly while savoring the delicious snack, so he figured the girls must make a lovely picture.

"They sure are cute, huh?" Itsuki remarked.

"No doubt, but they abandoned us to go flirt with each other," Amane replied.

"What, are you jealous?"

"Seeing two girls getting along isn't enough to make me jealous."

"Ha-ha, then just watch and enjoy. I think it's a fairly engaging scene, myself."

There was a lecherous tone to Itsuki's words as he mused on the delight of seeing two girls at play, but it wasn't like Amane didn't understand the feeling. He didn't want to seem like a pervert, though, so he swallowed his words as the two girls smiled chummily at each other.

Just then, from nearby, he heard a voice say "Miss Shiina?"

Amane turned around and saw several of their male classmates looking in Mahiru's and Chitose's direction.

It seemed they had also been enjoying the festival. They had masks on their heads and were holding bags of cotton candy, clearly having fun.

Itsuki was the first to react. He waved at them and walked over with his usual friendly, cheerful grin.

"Oh, you guys came to the festival, too, huh?"

"As soon as we saw Miss Shirakawa, we knew you'd be close by, Itsuki. Fujimiya, too."

"Right over here."

Amane didn't wave his hand in the air like Itsuki, but he did raise it casually, and when he did, a commotion started among the other boys.

"A *yukata*?" someone said.

"Something wrong with that?"

Amane smiled wryly. He could tell from his classmate's tone of voice that the other boy was surprised.

"No, it's just—you look like you know how to wear it…"

"I just put it on; that's all."

Aside from wearing a *yukata*, he wasn't doing anything special. There was nothing out of the ordinary, but to the other guys, it seemed like the presence of the *yukata* itself was special.

Amane felt unspeakably uncomfortable and itchy as they stared at him, and his face puckered up, but he relaxed again when he saw Mahiru leisurely walking over to him.

"Oh, it's been a while…," she said to their classmates. "Or maybe it hasn't been long enough to say that, but we haven't met since the closing ceremony, have we? I'm glad to see you all looking well."

"Whoa… Miss Shiina in a *yukata*…"

Amane fully expected every one of his classmates to be enchanted by the sight of his girlfriend, so he paid it no mind and continued gazing at her. She flushed slightly when she felt his eyes on her.

Just that was enough to freeze their classmates in place. Mahiru's adorableness was plain to see.

"M-miss Shiina, you look really great in a *yukata*."

"Thank you very much; I'm happy to hear you say so."

Mahiru must have only felt bashful receiving compliments when they came from Amane. Now she put on her beautiful public smile and merely accepted their praise.

"Did you put it on yourself?"

"Yes. Though, Amane's mother selected the *yukata* for me…"

"You don't need to worry one bit about the *yukata*," said Amane. "My mom would do pretty much anything to spoil you."

Amane's mother would probably pick out Mahiru's kimono for the new year, too. They had plenty of kimonos at the house, and even

more at Amane's maternal grandparents' house, so she would probably be delighted to do the choosing.

When he thought about being able to see Mahiru in yet another
kimono, Amane couldn't help but silently praise his mother.

"Still, I feel guilty for borrowing it."

"It's fine. My home is your home, right?"

His parents had told Mahiru that she could consider their home
her own, and they had certainly rolled out the welcome mat, so he figured they would be happier if she simply accepted the gesture.

Mahiru seemed to understand and nodded sheepishly as she
clutched her hands to her chest. Amane admired the sight, savoring a
mellow feeling of happiness, then glanced to one of their classmates
who had come over to talk to them.

*Come to think of it, this guy's one of the ones who turned on me back
on sports day.* He had remembered too late, but it hardly mattered
now.

No matter what, in Mahiru's mind, those boys were nothing
more than mere acquaintances. She wasn't going to let them come
between the two of them.

Amane silently chuckled at the feeling of superiority that gave
him. He knew it wasn't a good personality trait, but he had no intention of yielding any ground.

"Anyway, we don't want to interrupt your fun, so let's get going,"
Amane suggested. "Chitose's done eating her grilled squid, too," he
added, turning to Chitose, who was looking back at him with great
interest.

Amane casually drew Mahiru toward him with a hand around
her waist and flashed the other boys his usual smile.

Mahiru seemed surprised, but a clear delight showed through her
bashfulness, and she moved toward Amane of her own volition.

"Sure thing," she replied. "All right, I'll see you once summer break's over," she said to the other boys with a smile.

"Uh, y-yeah... Later."

Thanks to Mahiru, there was no way the boys could follow them around any longer. With disbelief written across their faces, they watched Amane and his friends take their leave.

Once they had left their classmates behind and started walking down the stall-lined road again, Itsuki came up to Amane on the opposite side from Mahiru and leaned toward him.

"Amane, you must have done that on purpose," he said.

Maybe he was trying to keep Mahiru from overhearing—his quiet voice disappeared into the hustle and bustle and festival music surrounding them.

"What part?"

"Oh, let's see. The way you're positioned now, for one, and that part about your home, too."

Itsuki really was a clever, perceptive guy. He had understood exactly what Amane had been implying—and why he'd been doing it.

"Who knows? Maybe I did, and maybe I didn't."

"...You've really toughened up, man," he muttered.

Itsuki's tone made it hard to tell if he was praising Amane or fed up with him. Amane decided to take it as a compliment and smiled meaningfully.

"Let's eat shaved ice next!"

The four friends, having resumed their tour of the festival, came to a stop once more at Chitose's proposal.

They had already passed the shaved ice stall.

There would probably be another one up ahead, but since they didn't know where it might be, it would be a little faster to go back, and it wasn't much of a bother to turn around.

More than anything, Amane was amazed that Chitose still had room.

"What kind of stomach do you have in there? Seriously..."

"This kind!"

Chitose playfully drummed her belly, but it looked just as slim as Mahiru's. Amane was surprised, since he knew it already contained *yakisoba*, fried chicken, and grilled squid.

Where does it all go...?

He was looking at her stomach with a serious expression when Mahiru grinned wryly. She must have been thinking the same thing.

"You never gain weight, do you, Chitose?" she said. "You're super slender; I'm jealous."

"It's a healthy kind of slenderness, though," Itsuki added. "She's all toned."

"Heh-heh, more compliments, please!"

"You really are slim, Chi... It's super easy to tell whenever I pick you up."

Itsuki often held her close, so he must have known just how slim Chitose was.

Itsuki wasn't particularly heavy himself—he was of medium build—and yet when they were clinging to each other, Chitose was noticeably thinner, which was saying something. It was obvious that she worked hard to maintain the perfect balance of slenderness and muscle.

"You eat a lot, but you never get fat, huh?"

"I've got a good metabolism."

"Yeah, and besides that, it's hard for you to put on weight with the way you're built. Although, that does mean you don't fill out in other places, either."

"...Itsuki, come over here."

Itsuki instantly realized he'd said too much when he heard Chitose speak to him in a monotone, despite her grin.

He had touched on an area that Chitose was quite sensitive about, so naturally she was angry. In fact, she seemed all the more angry because the comment had come from her boyfriend.

"I'm sorry; I didn't mean it; please don't kick me in the shins."

"You always have something to say, but that was one word too many! How about we have a little chat over there?" With a friendly grin, Chitose grabbed Itsuki's arm and pulled him away.

Amane watched Itsuki go, silently commiserating.

"Silence is golden, huh…?" he muttered.

"Did you say something?" Mahiru asked.

"Nope, not a thing."

Amane immediately denied it. He didn't need any repercussions coming his way. He forced himself to smile in an effort to keep Mahiru, who was looking troubled, from asking him to go rescue Itsuki.

"Mahiru, what flavor do you want?"

"Uh… S-strawberry milk…?"

"Okay, let's go get it. Chitose? We're gonna go ahead and get shaved ice, so you two play nice over there."

"Okaaay!"

Amane chuckled at Chitose, who turned back and answered with a smile even as she bullied Itsuki. Then Amane took Mahiru by the hand and headed back down the road.

Even after Amane and Mahiru had bought shaved ice and returned to their friends, Chitose's lecture was not over.

From a distance, Amane looked at the two of them, having an intimate discussion a little ways off the main road, and shrugged. Then he looked at Mahiru, who was clinging to his arm and exhibiting a strained smile.

"…Guess they're still going at it," he remarked.

"They're very close, aren't they?"

"I guess that's just another kind of flirting for them. Though Chitose does seem a little miffed."

"Ah, ah-ha-ha…"

Since he knew she wasn't truly angry, Amane didn't intervene. Instead, he handed Mahiru one of the cups of shaved ice he was holding.

"Here you go."

"Thank you very much. Amane…you look kind of glum."

"I really wanted an *ujikintoki* shaved ice, but of course the stall didn't have all the toppings."

Amane had chosen the green tea flavor.

If the shaved ice stall had had the toppings, he would have gone for the *ujikintoki*, but as one might expect, it was tough to find red beans and mochi balls at a festival stall, so he'd had no choice but to compromise.

"So you do eat sweets sometimes. You don't go for them very often, though."

"I don't dislike sweet foods; I just choose not to eat them. I do love red beans. Especially the coarse-ground kind."

He didn't usually go out of his way to eat sweet things, but he would if someone put them out. The only sweets he would seek out on his own were things like custard, and he didn't eat even those all that often, so he must have given off the impression that he didn't like such things.

The reason he enjoyed red beans was that they went well with bitter matcha and regular green tea. The bitter and sweet flavors enhanced one another, and he really appreciated the combination.

"Oh, do you? …Boiling down red bean paste is hard work, so it's a lot of trouble to make it."

"You're something else, Mahiru, to start thinking about it from the point of boiling the beans. The off-the-shelf stuff would be just fine…"

Most people would probably never even think of starting from the beans. Sweet red bean paste was sold in bags at the grocery store, so the overwhelming majority would simply use that, considering the time and effort required to make it from scratch.

But it seemed that, for Mahiru, the idea of making it by hand was what came naturally.

"Well, I like to make delicious food for the people I love. With the store-bought stuff, you can't really adjust the sweetness, and most of the time, they don't leave enough of the texture of the beans in."

Mahiru smiled and said admirably that she wanted Amane to eat what she made with gusto. Amane, feeling both guilt and joy at being so well loved, wasn't sure whether to relax into a smile or straighten up.

"…All right then, I want to eat matcha pudding garnished with sweet red bean paste. Also *dorayaki* pancakes."

"Heh-heh, fine," Mahiru said. "Just leave it to me! If it's for you, Amane, I'll make anything at all." She did not sound like she was exaggerating. Then she took a bite of her shaved ice.

Amane felt a wave of embarrassment, and in order to hide it, he scooped up a bite of his own shaved ice.

"Lucky you, matcha pudding!"

As they started eating, Chitose came over. She sounded jealous. Apparently, she had overheard their conversation while having her friendly chat with Itsuki.

"Are you done scolding Itsuki?"

"Of course. Geez, he can be so rude!"

Chitose gave them a thumbs-up, and Amane and Mahiru smiled at her, probably in unison. Amane looked over at the place where Itsuki had been a moment earlier, but…there was no one there.

"So where's Itsuki?"

"He went to buy shaved ice and a chocolate banana."

"The list keeps growing..."

"He's apologizing!"

Chitose turned away in a huff. Amane thought that Itsuki's wallet might end up empty, but at the same time, it was his own fault, so Amane didn't have too much pity for him.

Itsuki never learned, no matter how many times he stepped on the same land mine. But for the couple, this was probably one of the ways they bonded and communicated. Though it wasn't an ideal method, since it involved making one of them angry.

Chitose's sulking was lasting a little longer than usual, and she still had her lip stuck out in a pout. "It's not like they're small because I want them to be, geez. Why is it that guys all prefer curvy girls like you, Mahiru?"

Mahiru quickly covered her chest.

"I-I'm not sure what to say..."

Compared to Chitose, Mahiru's curves were dramatic. Amane was certain that she was curvier than average, but it would embarrass her if he paid too much attention to such things, so he had always tried not to stare.

"It's not like I hate you for it or anything, but I *am* jealous, you know? You've got plenty of things that I don't have, Mahiru. You're pretty, and you have a good figure, and you can handle schoolwork and sports and housework, and you're so ladylike... I think you're what most guys consider the ideal girl."

"That's not true."

"It is! I'm positive that if Daiki saw you, he'd tell Itsuki that he should have chosen a girl like you."

From the way Chitose was smiling dejectedly, Amane could more or less guess the reason that she had shown up unannounced at his and Mahiru's apartment building earlier that day.

166 * The Angel Next Door Spoils Me Rotten, Vol. 6

"Did Daiki say something to you?"

"Nah, he didn't say anything. It's just that the look in his eyes is never welcoming."

Daiki was Itsuki's father.

He was not happy about Itsuki and Chitose's relationship.

Amane had a chance to talk to him about it once, when he went to Itsuki's house. To put it simply, Daiki didn't care for Chitose's personality, and he wanted Itsuki to find himself a more typical girl, so he didn't look on Chitose very favorably.

He didn't hate Chitose, so much as believe that there was a different, better girl out there for his son.

"Daiki doesn't hate you or anything, you know."

"But if you put Mahiru in front of him, he would definitely choose her."

"W-well, I dunno…"

It was clear that Chitose had her own charms, including some that Mahiru lacked.

She was extremely cheerful and outgoing but also knew how to be polite when she needed to be—a girl who could truly read a room. She sometimes made deliberately silly statements, but she was also mature in many ways, and she always seemed to have a grasp on the big picture, so anyone with half a brain knew better than to underestimate her.

Considering both aspects of her personality, it was obvious she was no simple joker. But she wasn't the kind of person who Itsuki's father wanted for his son.

The kind of girl Daiki had in mind was an old-fashioned feminine beauty like Mahiru, and Chitose didn't check those boxes.

The ways in which Chitose didn't stack up weren't any fault of her own. It was simply a case of them being incompatible, with goals that didn't align.

Chitose sighed deeply, maybe because she was worried about Daiki not liking her.

"But even if I tried to be more like Mahiru…it would feel all wrong. Itsuki tells me I don't have to worry about it, but still, in the future, like, I want to become that man's daughter-in-law, right? I want to lay the foundation for a happy relationship."

"…That's tough. I don't think it's the kind of issue you can solve quickly."

"Yeah. It'll take years. Well, I'm trying, but it's hard when there's no progress. Some people just aren't compatible."

Chitose lamented with a smile that she would love to have official parental approval like Amane and Mahiru. Then she snuggled up to Mahiru and ate part of her shaved ice.

Amane wasn't sure what to say.

Mahiru must not have known, either. Instead, she gently patted Chitose's head.

Chitose leaned in to let her do it, begging for more shaved ice.

Just then, she saw through a gap in the crowd that Itsuki was coming back, holding the snacks she had ordered in both hands.

"I'm not all *that* bummed out about it, so don't say anything to Itsuki, okay?" Chitose said, cautioning them, then she headed toward Itsuki wearing her usual smile.

Amane and Mahiru watched her go, bewildered.

Once Itsuki returned from his errand, the group reunited. They then finished everything he had bought before going back to slowly wandering through the rows of stalls, moving with the flow of the people around them.

"Man, there sure are a lot of people," Amane remarked.

"That's because this is the only festival in the neighborhood,"

Itsuki told him. "There are extra food stalls, and the event itself is pretty big. We were bound to run into some guys from school."

Itsuki laughed cheerfully and added, "Though, they ran away with their tails between their legs!"

Amane was the one who had essentially driven them off, but he simply shrugged and left it there.

Mahiru overheard them, and she looked puzzled, probably wondering what Itsuki meant by *"ran away."*

Amane felt a small tickle of superiority at the fact that she must not have even been paying enough attention to them to notice.

I must be pretty possessive if I don't even want them to have her attention.

Amane had thought that the fact that Mahiru only had eyes for him was well-known due to her behavior at school, but apparently some guys just didn't know when to quit.

He understood how they felt.

This was a girl who was sweet and polished, everything a man could want. From the other boys' perspectives, it was probably hard to understand how some inexperienced nobody had swept her off her feet.

But he wished they would see how Mahiru obviously treated him differently from everyone else.

…I really am loved.

He'd already known that, of course, but recently he had come to feel it even more keenly.

He'd realized that he really was treasured and loved.

Naturally, Amane and Mahiru both put a lot of energy into their relationship, but it still made him uneasy how that brought him both embarrassment and pride at the same time.

"…You really do love Mahiru, don't you, Amane?" said Chitose. "It shows on your face."

"Huh?"

"Compared to before, you've gotten more sociable, and your expressions and the look in your eyes have softened... It feels weird to say it, but you've gotten a lot sweeter."

"...I'm aware that I've gotten a little more sociable, but I'm not sure how to respond to the idea that I've gotten sweeter..."

He could kind of tell that the way he acted and spoke had grown friendlier, but it was harder to for him to judge things like his expressions or the look in his eyes.

If anything, Amane thought he gave off an unfriendly impression, and he knew that he seemed like a cold person. So being told he was sweet puzzled him.

"Mahiru, am I that sweet?"

"Ah, w-well, um... Yes."

"Really? I'm not even sure what that would look like."

"I'll take a picture for you later, so you can see for yourself and agonize over it," said Itsuki, insisting that the change was really incredible.

Amane mused that he should try to refrain from being overly affectionate toward Mahiru in front of other people, but Mahiru was always so adorable that he wasn't confident he could hold back.

Mahiru's cheeks suddenly flushed red, and she glanced repeatedly over at him. For the time being, he stroked her cheek with his fingers. As he did so, he tried to put on a more serious expression.

"...It's a little late to be screwing up your face, man. You're not going to start fooling us now."

"Oh, hush."

"Mahiru, you must like Amane better when he's sweet, right?" said Chitose.

"Uh, w-well...um, I like all versions of Amane. I like him when he's sharply dressed, and I like him when he's sweet, and I like him when he's sexy..."

"Oh, so you've seen Amane looking sexy?"

Chitose shot him a sly grin, but Amane had absolutely nothing to feel guilty about, so while he grimaced back at her, he didn't get flustered.

Amane and Mahiru had been dating for over two months, and though they had finally gotten around to kissing, they hadn't gone any further than that. For the time being, they intended to take it slow.

Making those kinds of moves so soon after they started dating seemed wrong, like he was only interested in Mahiru for sex. Plus, Mahiru was the one who would have to deal with any consequences if they did do it, so it wasn't something he could casually set into motion.

It wasn't out of the question, if that was what Mahiru wanted. But at the moment, there was no indication that she did, so he saw no point in talking about it.

"We really don't do the sort of things you guys are imagining," Amane insisted.

"When you say that so confidently, it makes you sound a little repressed—or like your love is platonic or something."

"But you've kissed, right?" Chitose needled.

"…That's none of your business."

Amane lightly squeezed Mahiru's hand in his, as if to say *You told her something, didn't you?*

Mahiru turned bright red and mumbled quietly, "Sorry."

He couldn't complain, since he figured she must have mentioned it on an impulse during some girl talk, but he felt embarrassed having it pointed out like this.

Chitose must have felt they were taking it a little too slow. "You two sure are a couple of innocents," she said earnestly. "Either that or Amane's a total wuss."

Amane frowned. "…What's wrong with that?" he replied. "We're moving at our own pace."

"That's fine and all, but you know, if you make her wait too long, even a girl will get impatient! So you should probably get a move on."

"Chi-Chitose…"

"And you, Mahiru, it's best to tell it to him straight, okay? Rather than asking me for advice because Amane won't kiss you."

"Aaaaaaah, stop it! You can't just say things like that!"

As Mahiru tried to cover up Chitose's mouth, Amane's eyes went wide. Chitose, meanwhile, deftly avoided her friend's grasp, then gazed lovingly at the other girl.

However good Mahiru's reflexes were, Chitose's were better, and on top of that, unlike Mahiru, Chitose was wearing Western clothes, including pants, so it didn't seem like Mahiru had any hope of catching her.

"Heh-heh, you may be embarrassed, Mahiru, but I thought it was quite cute of you!" Chitose teased. "Though, it's true that I was a little exasperated with Amane for taking his sweet time."

"…If…if you say anything else, I won't help you with the last parts of your homework that you haven't finished!" Mahiru threatened.

"Can't have that. All right. My lips are sealed."

Chitose's face softened into an even wider smile at Mahiru's adorable threat. She drew her fingers across her lips, miming zipping them shut.

Mahiru was so embarrassed that she was trembling. Amane looked her in the eye, and when she noticed his gaze, her face went red again, and she seemed like she might run away. Amane grabbed her in a hurry.

He held her in place and patted her back to try to calm her down.

"You know that if we lose sight of each other, it'll be hard to meet back up, and someone will definitely hit on you, so stop trying to run away."

"…Urgh."

"I promise not to look at you, okay?"

He might not be looking, but he could feel her trembling in his arms. If he pointed that out, though, she might run away for real, so he kept it to himself as he reasoned with her.

Mahiru obediently settled into Amane's arms, still shaking.

The way she trusted him and did as he asked was cute, too. As he thought this, he could see Itsuki and Chitose looking at them with exasperation in their eyes.

"There it is—Amane's sweet face."

"He doesn't even realize he's doing it. How irritating."

Amane's cheek twitched as the two of them pretended to whisper to each other but deliberately spoke loudly enough for him to hear.

With Mahiru wrapped in his arms, however, he couldn't give them a piece of his mind. Instead, Amane switched out his "sweet" face for a new expression, making his dissatisfaction plain for all to see.

"Whew-wee, I sure did eat!"

"Where did you put all that…?"

The group had finished making the rounds, and Chitose was grinning with satisfaction as she rubbed her stomach.

Her belly looked a little more swollen than when they'd started, but she was still thin, and Amane wasn't sure whether he should be impressed or disturbed by how much she had managed to put away.

"Yup, the food at festivals like this is something special."

"Well, as long as you're satisfied, that's great, but…be careful not to eat too much."

"I hardly ever eat this much, and I'll make sure to work it all off!"

Chitose had long managed to maintain a slender physique, so he would have to take her word for it, though Amane couldn't help thinking she was overeating. But Chitose obviously knew what she was doing, and it wasn't his place to say anything.

"Actually, Amane, have you had enough? It feels like you've barely eaten anything."

"Mm… I was kind of planning to eat at home. Mahiru's got some dashi broth chilling, so I was thinking of making cold *chazuke* soup with that and some microwave rice."

"What? That sounds delicious."

"I can't believe you still feel like eating…"

Festival food was good, but Amane liked to finish off the day with Mahiru's cooking, so he hadn't eaten much. He was looking forward to using the dashi stock that Mahiru had left steeping to make his *chazuke*. He'd never imagined Chitose would still be hungry when he brought it up, though.

Faced with her friend's prodigious appetite, Mahiru forced a smile and chided her, "You can eat it some other time."

Just that day, they had seen her consume *yakisoba* and fried chicken, plus a hot dog and one of the octopus balls that Mahiru bought, followed by a chocolate banana and some shaved ice. It would have been enough to satisfy even a hungry guy, so Mahiru was probably worried about Chitose's stomach.

Amane looked at her slim hips, wondering where all that food had gone. Chitose must have noticed his gaze because she wiggled around and said teasingly, "You pervert!" He shot her a sour look in reply.

"Going forward, we'll have to keep an eye on Chitose's stomach capacity."

"Wow, you totally ignored me!"

"Okay, what should we do now? Ready to go home?"

They'd had their fun, and even though the sun set late in the summertime, the sky was already getting dark. It was going on eight thirty, so considering the transit time for Amane and Mahiru, whose apartments were far away, it was probably about time to wind things down. And while Chitose had Itsuki with her, it wasn't ideal for her to be out walking around too late, either.

"Sure, we can head back, but I'm staying at Mahiru's place, okay?" Chitose answered.

"Huh?"

"I already left my bags there, and I got permission from your better half before we came out! Right?" Chitose grinned at Mahiru, who put on a wry smile and nodded.

Mahiru didn't look put out, so Amane wasn't worried. But if possible, he would have preferred that she say something earlier. Amane was the one who did the grocery shopping, so if there were going to be three of them, he needed to provide three people's worth of food.

"I wish I had asked Amane about staying over, too," Itsuki said to his grinning girlfriend. He sounded disappointed. It was kind of pitiful to think about him returning home alone, but he had no change of clothes, so there was nothing he could do.

"...Well, if Mahiru says it's okay, then I guess it's okay."

"Oh no, Amane, are you cranky because I'm stealing Mahiru away?"

"Why would I be jealous of a girl? I know that Mahiru's mine, so it's fine by me."

More than being upset about Chitose hanging all over Mahiru, Amane was jealous of how, as another girl, she could be so carefree about going in and out of Mahiru's apartment.

Mahiru had already promised to let him come over, but he still needed time to mentally prepare, and so he envied Chitose, who could do it effortlessly.

So Amane shrugged and insisted that it was much too late to feel jealous of Chitose.

But Mahiru flushed red and quickly retreated over to Chitose, whispering in her friend's ear. "…This is what I was talking about. Recently, Amane has started acting like this…"

"Oh my, I can see how that would make things tough for you," Chitose replied.

"What's with that look?" Amane demanded.

"Nothing!" Chitose smiled impishly, this time a little different from when she'd asked for Mahiru's permission earlier. "Right, Mahiru?"

Mahiru bobbed her head in a silent nod and leaned in close to Chitose, looking bashfully in Amane's direction.

"Amaneee, let's play a game!"

"Why are you calling right before bed…?"

Chitose ended up spending the night at Mahiru's place, so after the festival, Amane had spent the rest of the evening on his own. But just before bed, a video call had come in from Chitose, causing him to frown.

It wasn't that he hated getting calls, but a video call just as he was lying down and sleepily settling into bed was a bit annoying.

On the screen was a close-up of Chitose's grinning face, which was already an irritating intrusion, Amane thought somewhat rudely. He moved his phone away and set it next to his pillow.

"Listen, Chitose," he said, "I was about to go to sleep."

"Yeah, I know. I can tell from how you're dressed and the fact that you're lying down."

"If you've understood, then can I hang up?"

"No way. At least wait until Mahiru gets back!"

"Now that you mention it, where is Mahiru?"

"In the baaath. She wouldn't get in with me today; can you believe it?"

Chitose sounded disappointed, but Mahiru had made the right decision.

Bathing together would have been exhausting. Mahiru would not have been able to relax at all, so getting in alone had surely been the better choice.

"Mahiru was all bummed that she wouldn't get to say good night to you. That's why I called you like this. So, Amane, don't hang up yet!"

"...Now that you've said that, I guess I can't, huh?"

"Are you saying you would have if I didn't say anything? Geez, what a meanie!" Chitose cackled with laughter. Then she abruptly put on a serious face and stared at Amane through the screen.

There was nothing left of her teasing attitude from a moment earlier. She was wearing a calm and somewhat philosophical expression. Amane couldn't help but feel bewildered at the sudden change.

"Hey, Amane, can I ask you something?"

"What?"

The change in her expression told him that a serious question was coming, so he responded in kind rather than dismissing her.

Chitose's eyes bored into him.

"Amane, how much do you love Mahiru?"

"How much?"

"You seem to really treasure her, so I was wondering, how much do you love her?"

He frowned at the difficult question, but Chitose's expression didn't change.

"...Maybe this is just bias on my part, but hmm, aren't relationships usually—I mean, high school relationships—usually just like, temporary fun? Less serious and more like a game."

"Did Itsuki's father tell you that?"

"Whoa! You're pretty sharp, huh?"

Chitose put on a foolish grin, but there was no spirit in her smile, and to Amane, it looked a little like she was depressed.

He watched her sigh softly and roll across the bed without ever letting go of her phone.

"...*It's not like I plan on just playing around for a little while or anything. But I'm always smiling like an idiot, so no one takes me seriously, you know? Maybe that's why... I'm curious to know if there are other people who are looking way ahead into the future.*"

She had let them see a little glimpse of it at the festival, but in her own way, Chitose must have been putting in a lot of work to figure out how to compromise with Itsuki's father. Itsuki's mother seemed indifferent to that aspect of her son's life, so his father was the one Chitose had to overcome.

Amane took his time before answering Chitose's question.

But in the end, his answer didn't require much thought.

"...It's difficult for me to say how much I love her, but...my intention is to keep her by my side and make sure she's always smiling."

It was hard to describe how much he loved Mahiru. He wasn't sure what he could liken his feelings to.

The only thing he was certain of was that he wanted to make her happy, to treasure her and make her smile, and to be by her side for the rest of his life. Those sentiments filled his heart.

"...*Gotcha.*"

"Do you not feel that way, Chitose?"

"*That's not what I mean,*" Chitose answered. She sounded a little annoyed. "*I want to make Itsuki laugh his head off for the rest of his life; of course I do.*"

"Mm, I think that's good enough," Amane answered with a smile. "If you say so, then that's how it is, and nothing's gonna change because of what somebody else says."

On the other side of the screen, Chitose winced.

"…You're, like, way too good of a guy. It's irritating."

"I'm dating a great girl; shouldn't I want to be a great guy?"

"Ugh, and listen to that confidence… You make me sick!"

If Chitose had been in the room with him, he probably would have gotten a vigorous slap on the back. That's how much annoyance he could hear in her voice… But he could hear a hint of happiness as she grumbled *"Mahiru really is loved, isn't she?"* before breaking into a smile.

Then she turned around.

In that same moment, Amane heard a familiar voice ask, *"What are you talking about in here?"*

He could see that Mahiru was finished with her bath. She was standing behind Chitose, dressed in a nightgown that showed very little skin.

Amane told himself it wasn't right to stare at girls in their nightclothes and subtly shifted his gaze away from them, though it wasn't a very convincing argument considering he'd just been looking at Chitose in her pajamas. Now looking away, he pricked up his ears.

Mahiru must have approached Chitose. Something flaxen-colored fluttered at the edge of the screen.

"Hmm? I was just saying what a great guy your boyfriend is, Mahiru."

"Is something up with Amane?"

"I was just getting some life advice from him."

"Life advice…?"

"Uh-huh."

Chitose's reply was technically true, and on the other side of the screen, Mahiru let out a small sigh at her friend.

Slightly taken aback by Mahiru's attitude, Chitose huffed in displeasure before Amane saw Mahiru sit down next to her.

"…You didn't want to get advice from me?" Mahiru asked. She sounded a little sulky.

©Hanekoto

Chitose stiffened, and the very next moment, she tossed her phone aside.

Amane's view through the smartphone went spinning, but through the speaker, he could hear Mahiru shriek in her delicate voice, so he figured they had probably moved on to Chitose's specialty, which was cuddling.

"...Mahiru, you're so cute! I'm coming for you; I can't be stopped!"

"Chitose... It's dangerous to jump on me!" Mahiru chided.

But there was happiness in her voice, so she probably wasn't as upset as she would have Chitose believe.

Amane heard Chitose giggle. *"Eh-heh!"* The front camera of her smartphone must have been buried in the bedsheets because the screen was blacked out, but Amane could imagine that Chitose was clinging tightly to Mahiru.

"Mahiru, I love you!"

"I love you, too."

"Heh-heh! I stole Mahiru's love away from Amane!"

"Huh? A-Amane is, well, he's in his own category...!"

Mahiru picked up the phone and desperately tried to explain in a panicked voice, making Amane crack a little smile.

"I already know that much."

"...Oh."

"You know, you guys are just as bad as any cringey couple."

"Hush. We're just copying you."

Chitose and Itsuki were just as cringey, so he didn't want to hear any criticism from either of them.

"Go on, finish up your slumber party and hurry to bed; I thought staying up late was bad for the skin."

They'd reached a good stopping point, so Amane cut off things there.

The clock showed it was already past eleven PM. He knew that

Mahiru, who didn't stay up very late, would probably drift off before too long. She had been walking around in a *yukata*, which she wasn't used to, so she was probably worn out, and it was about time for her to start getting sleepy.

In fact, ignoring the redness in her cheeks, Mahiru, who was holding Chitose's smartphone, looked ready to drift off, so it didn't seem right to drag the call on too long.

"*I never thought I would hear something like that from you,*" Chitose remarked. "*Well, I guess you've got a point; it's about time we hang up... Hey, Mahiru, is that okay?*"

At Chitose's urging, Mahiru, who seemed to have realized why Chitose had called her boyfriend, opened her eyes in surprise. Then she looked at Amane and smiled gently.

"*Oh...sure. Good night, Amane. See you tomorrow.*"

"Yeah, sleep well. See you tomorrow."

Amane thought about how, if she were beside him, he would have liked to stroke her head, but he wanted Chitose and Mahiru to enjoy themselves that evening, so he didn't let his feelings show on his face. Instead, he smiled back at the two girls, who seemed to be enjoying their sleepover, and bid them good night.

Chapter 8

Finish Your Homework First

"Amane, help me!"

"Nope."

Chitose was sitting at the living room table holding her mechanical pencil. Amane didn't bother to hide his exasperation as he rejected her cry for help.

Chitose had spent the night at Mahiru's, apparently with the intention of finishing her summer assignments.

Perhaps in an attempt to get Amane involved, too, she had decided, without asking, to do her work at his apartment and had come over for that purpose. But Amane had finished his assignments nearly a month earlier and was just doing some self-study, so he was in no hurry to join her.

There was no reason for him to rush over to the table, so instead, he sat on the sofa leafing through a magazine, occasionally looking over at Chitose.

"First of all, this is your fault for putting off your work and not finishing it. You've got to plan ahead. I think it's much better to work hard early on and finish your assignments, then have fun for the rest of summer vacation, than to find yourself in a bind at the end and close out the holidays tired and in a bad mood."

"Ugh."

"You could have done it together with Itsuki. He already finished his assignments, too, and he even worked at it little by little. If you had done the same thing, you wouldn't be struggling now."

"Ugggh."

"In fact, why are you so sure that you can just rely on other people to help you get it done? You're the one who has to solve the problems. Your laziness is just coming back to bite you, and the quickest way to get it over with is to quit floundering around, pull up to the table, and do the work."

"Mahiruuu, Amane's bullying meee!"

Amane had thought he was making a sound argument, but now Chitose was whining to Mahiru.

Mahiru had just poured her friend some juice, and she came in carrying a tray with glasses full of orange liquid on it.

"You shouldn't be so harsh with her, Amane."

Mahiru smiled wryly as she chided Amane before passing him a glass of orange juice.

"See!" Chitose said. Mahiru's reinforcement had gotten her worked up, and she shot Amane a look that said he ought to follow his girlfriend's example.

However, Mahiru was not completely on Chitose's side, either. If anything, her way of thinking was closer to Amane's, which was why she had finished her assignments early and had already moved on to independent study.

It was Mahiru's style to steadily work away at her assignments, but she had already finished all her summer homework. No matter the task, it wasn't much fun to be hounded by deadlines, so she got done what she needed to do and then reviewed so as not to forget the material.

Amane was relieved that her line of thinking was basically the same as his own.

"Heh-heh, if only the old Amane who didn't know how to pick up after himself could hear you say that," she teased.

"Uh, well, about that..."

Though his was a different type of laziness, once Mahiru delivered this blow of sound logic, Amane couldn't say anything more.

"Oh, she really told you!" Chitose cackled when she saw that Mahiru had shut him up.

Mahiru had just set a glass of orange juice down on the table. She smiled gently at the amused Chitose, then slowly placed her hand on her friend's shoulder.

"Putting all that aside, Chitose, you'd better get to work, okay?"

"Not you, too, Mahiru! Weren't you on my side?!"

"I *am* on your side. But that doesn't mean you don't have work to do. I asked you at the beginning of summer vacation if you wanted to do the assignments together, but you decided to slack off..."

"Ugggh."

"This is nothing but the consequences of your own actions."

Chitose had chosen to play around, despite Mahiru's invitation, which didn't exactly invite sympathy.

"Chitose, you may have a lot of homework left, but I'm here with you, so you'll be fine."

"Mahiru...!"

"Right now, if you work at the table until dinner, you can get about halfway through it... Right?"

"Nooo!"

Mahiru sent Chitose spiraling into despair by snipping, with natural ease, the spider's thread of hope that the other girl was reaching for.

Amane looked over at Chitose and commented "Poor thing" with an air of indifference, before taking a sip of the orange juice he had been given.

He was tentatively prepared to swap in for Mahiru if Chitose was really stumped, or more likely if Mahiru got tired of coaching her, but Chitose would never learn if they babied her too much, so they were trying to be firm with her.

Chitose whined and moaned, but still she reluctantly prepared to do her work. Amane looked on from the side, as he considered going out to buy her something sweet later.

"I'm. So. Tiiired!"

Chitose had been frantically working away at her assignments, taking short breaks along the way, but as one might have expected, it eventually wore her out. She flopped down and rolled around on the carpet like she was throwing a tantrum.

It was fine because she was wearing shorts that day, but she was moving in a way that would have revealed her underwear had she been wearing a skirt. Amane watched her with unconcealed dismay.

"What are you gonna do if you spill juice or something with all that flailing around?" he asked.

"If that happens, I'll just have to throw myself on your mercy."

"Rather than throw away your pride, you should try harder not to spill things in the first place. Besides, it would suck if the carpet and your clothes got dirty, right?"

Mahiru was considerately holding their two cups, which had been sitting on the table, so there was nothing to worry about, but if she had let them be, an accident might have occurred.

Amane wouldn't have been angry about juice spilling on the carpet, but considering the time and effort it would take to remove the stain, he still didn't want Chitose to spill any.

"You should try to act more like an adult," Mahiru chimed in.

Mahiru's smile was a little strained, but she didn't seem inclined to put a stop to Chitose's behavior. She probably knew that if she didn't let her friend relax a little, she would get worn out.

"Hmm, well, since there's nowhere for me to lie down, I'm moving to Mahiru's lap!"

"Hold up; that's my special reserved seat."

"So stingy. Mahiru, can I?"

"…If Amane says no, then the answer is no."

Mahiru cast her eyes down and slowly shook her head a little awkwardly.

At this, Chitose didn't show the slightest bit of dissatisfaction at being rejected and put on a broad grin instead. "I may not get to use your lap as a pillow, but as long as you look happy, that's good enough for me."

Mahiru looked more embarrassed than happy, but her cheeks, though flushed, had curved into a smile, so maybe Chitose was right.

Maybe the words *special reserved seat* had made Mahiru happy.

"All right then. You better hurry up and enjoy your spot in my place, Amane. It'll inspire me to do my work."

"Not a chance. You'd definitely tease me for it. I know it's mine, so I'll enjoy it when you're not around."

"I bet you will."

"I'm allowed—it's my special privilege. Anyway, I'm gonna go buy you something sweet, so get to it and do your work."

"Really?!"

Chitose jumped to her feet, her eyes sparkling with excitement. Her reaction drove home the fact that she was easily bribed.

188 * The Angel Next Door Spoils Me Rotten, Vol. 6

It was clear from her smile that she'd been waiting for those words. Both Amane and Mahiru broke out in wry grins.

"It's your reward," Amane said. "If you sit down and work seriously, I'll go buy something for you right now."

"I will, I will! That's just like you, Amane, so generous! Something from my regular shop would be great! A cheesecake, okay? One of the soufflé ones!"

"I didn't expect you to put in an order... Well, it's not that far away, so I guess it's fine, but..."

Compared to the cake shop nearby, Chitose's favorite spot was a little farther away, and its prices were a little higher. It wasn't terribly expensive, though, and Mahiru also seemed to like the cakes there, so Amane had no objection about going.

"And for you, Mahiru?"

"Huh, for me...?"

"If you're going to buy for everyone, why doesn't Mahiru go with you?"

"Because you'll slack off, so she can't leave. Besides, it would be wrong to make her walk in the blazing sun."

"It's incredible how little faith you have in me... But you're a gentleman, Amane, so I'll be generous and swallow my feelings this time."

"If you keep this up, I'm not going to get you anything."

"Won't that defeat the purpose of going...?"

"Well then, hush. And get to work on those assignments."

Chitose looked at him like she couldn't believe what she was hearing, but he ignored it and asked Mahiru what she wanted. He got his answer—gâteau chocolate—and stood up to leave.

He expected that demand for cakes was lower during the summer season, but it wasn't impossible that they would be sold out. It would probably be best to go early.

"All right, I'm off."

Amane left the living room with his wallet in hand and Mahiru trailing gracefully behind him.

Apparently, she planned to walk him out. As Amane sat on the entryway ledge and put on his sneakers, Mahiru crouched down on her knees beside him.

"What's up?" he asked.

"Nothing, I just feel bad sending you out in the heat…"

"It's fine; I'm the one who suggested it. You have the more-important job of watching over Chitose."

"Heh-heh, Chitose is a little childish at times, but when she puts her mind to it, she can be very serious, you know?"

"Yeah, but still… Be clever about taking breaks and get her to work hard, okay?"

"Roger that."

Mahiru let a giggle slip out as she nodded in agreement, and Amane smiled back at her as he stood up.

"Well then, be back soon."

"Ah, hang on, Amane, can you wait a minute?"

She called out to stop him, and when he turned around, Mahiru suddenly leaned against his chest.

When he stiffened at the sudden movement, Mahiru stirred restlessly and put her arms around his back, pulling her body tight against his.

He almost let out a groan at the sweet scent that gently drifted up from her and the soft feeling of her body. Somehow enduring the sensation, he stroked Mahiru's head for lack of anything better to do, and she looked up at him, her eyes narrowed as if his touch tickled.

"…I'm a little worn out from all the studying today, so I needed to replenish my reserves," she whispered quietly.

©Hanekoto

Unable to bear it any longer, Amane embraced Mahiru back. He saw a shy look in her eyes, but at the same time, she was smiling happily.

"...When you say stuff like that, it makes me never want to let go."

"That would be a problem. Chitose would be sad."

"...How about after Chitose goes home?"

"I'd love nothing more."

Mahiru nodded and buried her head in Amane's chest once more, and Amane pledged in his heart to finish his errand and return home quickly.

He discovered the letter on his way back from buying cakes for the girls, when he peeked into his mailbox in the lobby.

Mixed in with the usual advertising flyers was a single unfamiliar envelope.

On it, his name was written in neat letters, *Mr. Amane Fujimiya*. He turned it over calmly, wondering who on earth would have sent such a thing and couldn't believe what he saw.

The name of the sender was written on the back.

Asahi Shiina.

...That must be Mahiru's father.

He had heard that her mother's name was Sayo, so it wasn't from her.

What's more, Mahiru's father was probably the only one who knew about Amane.

He must have seen them that time when Mahiru came down to meet him in the lobby. It wouldn't have taken much digging to figure out that Amane was close with Mahiru.

But Amane couldn't think of a reason why the man would go out of his way to send him a letter. Why would he send a letter not to his daughter, but to his daughter's boyfriend?

According to Mahiru, her father had no interest in her. That was what she had said, but if he really wasn't interested, he wouldn't have come to see how she was doing.

Amane didn't have a clue what Mahiru's father was after. He was at a complete loss.

He decided to go back to his apartment for the time being, then open the letter after Chitose left. With that settled, he tucked the envelope away in his bag.

"You've been acting strangely ever since you got back, Amane. Did something happen?"

Once Chitose had finished about 70 percent of her homework, moaning all the while, and gone home, Mahiru peered at Amane's face questioningly.

Amane had considered opening the letter after Mahiru went home, but she seemed to have realized he was hiding something.

It wasn't that he wanted to hide it, he just didn't know what might be written in the letter, so he had decided that it would be best not to carelessly tell Mahiru about it. But if she was going to suspect him, he would rather tell her right from the start.

"Ah, well, how should I put it—?"

"Oh... Um, if you don't want to tell me, I won't force you to."

Apparently, Mahiru was ready to respect Amane's wishes absolutely. He looked at her as he uncrossed his legs.

"It's not exactly that I don't want to tell you," he said, "more like you probably won't want to hear it."

"I won't want to hear it...? Ah, so that's what it is."

She must have realized that it had something to do with her parents because the next moment, a faint, bitter smile crossed her lips.

"Don't tell me that man was here again?"

"No, it's not that. But…there was a letter, addressed to me."

"Addressed to you? From who?"

"…The name Asahi Shiina was written on it."

"That'll be my father, then," Mahiru said, nodding readily.

She didn't seem as upset as Amane had expected. She seemed detached—not shocked, just a little bit surprised.

He did, however, detect a slight frostiness in her gaze, probably due to the treatment she'd received from her parents.

"I do wonder why he sent a letter to you, and how he knew about our relationship, but I don't suppose that's any of my concern."

"Aren't you curious about what it says?"

"I don't make a habit of looking at other people's mail," Mahiru declared decisively. "The letter may be from my father, but it's addressed to you, Amane."

At that point, Amane realized that he had been so worried about Mahiru, but she was more preoccupied with looking out for him.

And yet rather than accepting the letter for what it was, she seemed instead to want nothing to do with it.

She appeared only just a little less composed than usual as she shifted her gaze about the room and said in a chilly voice, "If you're going to read it, go ahead. Would you like me to leave?"

Amane flashed her a small, strained smile and shook his head. "Hmm… I'm not sure how to put this, but I guess I want you beside me. If you don't want to stay, I can look at it myself, but I'm kind of nervous about getting a letter from my girlfriend's father."

"In that case, I'll be right here… I'll leave it up to you whether to tell me what's in the letter."

Mahiru picked up a textbook from the table and started to read. Amane sighed softly, then pulled the envelope out of his bag, which had been sitting beside him.

He carefully opened the envelope, which was glued tightly shut. He took out the stationery from inside it, then scanned the words written on the paper.

To summarize, the letter said that Mahiru's father wanted to get together and talk. He had included his contact information.

...Why is he sending this to me?

Maybe he hadn't come to see how Mahiru was doing, after all. Amane had absolutely no idea why her father would reach out to him, a person with whom he had basically no connection.

"...I guess, it seems like he wants to meet me."

"Not his daughter, but you? Is that so?"

Mahiru's voice had turned even chillier, so on instinct, he stroked her head, and she narrowed her eyes as if his touch had tickled her.

"I mean, I'm not angry or anything...," she said. "I genuinely don't understand what he's planning. I don't know why he wants to meet up with you."

"...Normally, I'd assume it's because I'm dating his daughter, or something, but..."

"Not likely. I can't imagine him interfering at this stage, when he's neglected me up until now."

"...What do you think I should do?"

"I don't care; I don't have any intention of keeping you from seeing him." Her words were very frank—she really did seem inclined to leave it up to Amane. "Oh, and if you're worried that meeting him might put you in danger, I don't think you need to be concerned. I don't think he's qualified to be a parent, but otherwise I believe he's a sensible person—and not someone who would try to threaten you or anything... Though, that might sound strange, coming from someone who hardly knows anything about him."

"...Mahiru."

"I don't know what he's scheming, but he's not the type of person who would hurt someone, so you can rest assured about that. You're free to go or not go, whatever you want."

After Mahiru finished speaking, she leaned against him, as if putting herself in Amane's hands.

"Okay," he answered quietly, before looking at the letter one more time.

Chapter 9

A Once-Desired, Now Undesired Meeting, and a Resolution

It was the last day of summer vacation.

If it were any other year, Amane would have been resting at home, not going anywhere. That was even more true now that he had Mahiru. But on that day, Amane was headed out.

He got himself ready, dressing up enough so he wouldn't offend the person he was meeting, then headed for the agreed-upon place.

...I hope this doesn't take too long.

He wasn't nervous about talking to someone he didn't know. He was worried that the longer the conversation dragged on, the more anxious Mahiru would get.

Mahiru had feigned composure when he told her that he was going to meet her father, but he knew there was no way she felt good about it. It was obvious that she was worried about what her father might say—and what Amane would think of him.

Amane didn't want to leave Mahiru alone in that state for longer than he needed to, and so he was determined to ascertain the other man's real intentions as quickly as possible.

Weighed down by a great deal of emotion, Amane plodded toward the meeting place. Then, as he approached the café—not far from his apartment building—he spotted the person he was there to meet and straightened up.

Standing before Amane was a gentle-looking, fair-skinned man with flaxen hair and caramel-colored eyes, just like the ones he was used to seeing every day.

It was the same man he had crossed paths with once before—and with whom he had made light conversation. They hadn't exchanged names, but Amane had heard his from Mahiru, and so he knew who he was.

"Mr. Asahi Shiina?"

When Amane spoke the man's name, he—Asahi Shiina—turned to look at Amane, and a faint smile appeared on his face.

"Nice to meet you...," he said. "Well, it's not really our first meeting, but this is the first time we've had a conversation where we both know who the other is."

"...I suppose so. I've heard a little about you from Mahiru."

The man didn't appear shaken by Amane casually calling Mahiru by her first name, so he had probably looked into their relationship.

In response, Asahi's thin smile grew slightly strained. He gave the impression of being calm, not timid, and at first glance, he didn't seem like the kind of monster who would have neglected Mahiru as a child. Though, appearances could be deceiving, and this was still only a first impression.

"In that case, we can get right to it," Asahi said. "Could I have a little bit of your time?"

"That's why you asked me here, isn't it?" Amane replied.

"Indeed. I'm very grateful you accepted my sudden request. Though I asked, I never expected you to agree."

"I was wondering why you went out of your way to contact me... Shouldn't you be meeting with Mahiru instead?"

Amane wasn't sure about Asahi's intentions, and although he

realized he ought to be acting friendly toward him, he just couldn't resist giving the man a small piece of his mind.

Asahi seemed to understand what Amane was implying, and he frowned uncomfortably. "When you put it that way, you're right, but…I'm sure that she doesn't want to see me," he said.

With a wry smile, Asahi seemed filled with regret.

Amane was angry with him on Mahiru's behalf. He didn't think he would be able to forgive him. But the man before him didn't seem like a heartless monster. If he was, surely he wouldn't have gone out of his way to, however indirectly, quietly make contact with his daughter.

Amane's doubts were only growing.

Why wasn't he meeting directly with Mahiru—and instead beating around the bush by reaching out to someone close to her?

Amane still didn't know what he was thinking or what he wanted out of this.

Asahi must have noticed the quizzical look in Amane's eyes. He scratched his cheek and smiled awkwardly.

"You must also have plenty of things you want to ask me, right? We can't have a long conversation out here, so how about we go into the café?"

Indeed, there was no way they could have a deep conversation standing out on the street, so Amane agreed and walked into the café with him.

"Order whatever you like. I'm the one who called you out here on the last day of your precious summer vacation, after all."

The café, which Amane had visited from time to time, had private rooms that were available by reservation. Asahi must have reserved one in advance because they were shown through to one of them.

As soon as they sat down across from each other, Asahi offered him a menu, a gentle smile on his face.

Amane said he would take him up on his offer and informed him that he would have the daily special cake plate that came with coffee, as listed on the menu. Asahi ordered the same thing.

Then Asahi sat with that same gentle expression on his face and didn't open his mouth until their orders were delivered.

Amane figured he was probably keeping quiet because he didn't want the staff to overhear their conversation. But for Amane, sitting across from a man not all that different in age from his own father, the situation felt extremely awkward.

In order to distract himself, he mentally organized the things he wanted to ask that day, and around the third time he repeated the exercise, their orders were finally placed in front of them.

After making sure the waiter had left, Amane spoke up.

"So what business do you have with me?"

It was a bit rude to ask so suddenly, but Asahi only smiled. He did not seem offended.

"Of course. It seems you are dating my daughter, so I wanted to ask you how she is getting along... I suppose that's the best way to put it."

"...She's doing all right."

"I can tell you're wary of me."

"Did you think I wouldn't be?"

"Of course not; it would be strange if you weren't."

Asahi nodded, and Amane pursed his lips. He was not sure how to respond.

If, for example, Asahi had been as cruel to his daughter as Mahiru's mother was, Amane could have put on a strong front and dealt with the situation in any number of ways.

But the sense Amane was getting from Asahi was that he was worried about his daughter. He really didn't seem like the type to abandon his child. Based only on this single conversation, he seemed to be a decent father.

That made Amane wonder exactly why he had deserted Mahiru.

It was certainly possible that he was putting on a friendly face—and that he might change the moment he secured an opportunity to make contact with Mahiru. But Amane's intuition was telling him that wasn't the case.

"I'd like to ask you something myself. Why is it that you're going out of your way at this point to try to get closer to Mahiru?"

It was because Amane had seen how deeply Mahiru had been wounded by her father that he found it so disagreeable that the man would show up now, of all times.

No matter how many years had passed, the thorn of hurt that had pierced his daughter's heart had never come out, and she had been suffering this whole time.

Recently, that thorn had only just begun to work its way loose and the wound had started to heal, so the thought of letting her be hurt anew was intolerable.

Amane, who intended to spend his life beside her, didn't want her to suffer any unnecessary hurt. He refused to let her experience any needless pain.

As long as he and Mahiru were moving forward together, supporting one another, if it was possible to prevent such injury, he would do it, and if he could protect her from danger, he intended to do that, too.

"...You really do take good care of that girl, don't you?"

Asahi simply seemed impressed. He looked at Amane with a pleased expression—and without returning any of the hostility directed at him.

"I'm not thinking of trying to take her back with me or anything. You seem to be worried, but I don't intend to do anything to threaten her life here."

"...Really?"

"Of course... I have no right to interfere with the life she has now. I'm not even considering it."

"So then why are you really attempting to make contact with Mahiru?"

"...When you put it that way, it's hard to explain. I just came to see her face."

"Even though you're the one who abandoned her?"

Amane was fully aware that this was not something that a stranger, an outsider like him, should say.

And yet the treatment Mahiru had suffered at the hands of her parents was unforgivable.

Because of them, Mahiru had been continuously hurt, and in order to hide her pain, she had put on the mask of a charming, perfect girl. She had reached out for them, begging to be loved.

So why was someone who had never once rewarded Mahiru for her attempts to reach him turning his eye on her now?

If he was reaching out to her on a whim, Amane wanted to brush off his hand. Though some might say Amane was acting out of self-ish resentment, he intended to pull Mahiru away from anything that might cause her tears or pain.

Surprisingly, Asahi was showing Amane respect. He did not look angry, and he simply met Amane's gaze with a calm expression.

"You like to get right to the point, don't you?"

Even if the older man had been angry at him, the only thing he showed Amane was that calm expression, which fueled the fire of Amane's fury.

To keep from exploding, he was balling up his hands tightly underneath the table, channeling his impulses into his fists.

"You're correct, of course. At this point, I don't have any right to act like a parent. It's questionable whether she even still considers me to be her father. I bet she probably thinks of me more like a stranger to whom she's related by blood."

"…If you're aware of that, you must also understand what you did to her."

"I'll never be able to escape from what I did, for as long as I live… Sayo and I failed to live up to our roles as her parents. I'm sure that people would call the way we treated her neglect. It's only natural that she blames us."

Asahi coolly took an objective view of his and his wife's misdeeds. Amane chewed on his lower lip.

Why not earlier?

Why couldn't he have reflected on his actions earlier?

If he'd been able to do that, Mahiru wouldn't have been as hurt as she was. Even if she hadn't been able to get any love from her mother, she might have received it from her father. She might have been happy.

Why is he repenting now?

Amane didn't know where he should direct his anger.

He probably wasn't entitled to be angry. His rage was probably unreasonable.

Even so, it bubbled up inside him.

Amane couldn't help but wonder why this man hadn't extended a hand to his daughter sooner.

If they had been outside, he might have raised his voice and grabbed Asahi by the collar. But Amane kept his cool, knowing that he mustn't cause an uproar in the café and risk letting strangers know they were talking about Mahiru. After considering what might happen, he resisted making a fuss.

It had been a brilliant tactic on Asahi's part to choose this place.

"Do you know what she said? Mahiru said that if she was such an

204 The Angel Next Door Spoils Me Rotten, Vol. 6

inconvenience, she never should have been born… You and your wife drove her to say that."

"…Indeed."

Amane spoke in a flat, dead serious voice as he somehow managed to keep from shaking. All the while, Asahi's eyes seemed to fully understand and accept everything he was saying.

The man's reaction only aggravated Amane more.

"If you were going to neglect Mahiru and then feel bad about it so much later, you should have committed yourself to her from the beginning. If you had done that, she wouldn't have been hurt so badly."

"There's nothing I can say to that… Of course, I'm fully aware that I've done the worst thing a parent can do."

"…In that case, really, why now…? Why are you trying to see her now? If meeting you will only hurt Mahiru, I don't want to let you see her. I know I'm only an outsider, but if it's just going to upset her, I don't want it to happen."

There was no way he could interfere with a meeting between a father and daughter. But Mahiru didn't want to see the man, so Amane found himself speaking emphatically.

Even if the man reproached him, Amane didn't intend to yield.

Asahi accepted Amane's pointed look with a bitter, apologetic smile.

"Why do I want to see her? …I suppose I'm not sure."

"Are you dodging the question?"

"I don't mean to. It's just—it's quite difficult to put into words, you know? …I suppose…I thought I'd try to see her while I still can."

"Does that mean that you won't be able to see her in the future? Or maybe that you don't intend to?"

"That's right."

A bitter taste welled up in Amane's mouth at the confirmation.

"…You're a selfish man."

"You're right, I am selfish. And I don't intend to change, nor do I think I could at this point. But I don't want to cause my daughter any more unhappiness, either. So it's probably for the best that she hates me."

"I don't understand what you mean."

"You will, sooner or later."

From the meaningful look in Asahi's eyes, Amane could tell that he didn't intend to say any more on the matter, and so he gave up pressing him.

"Is there anything else you want to ask me?" Asahi asked.

"…No, I'm good."

"I see… Well then, would you allow me to ask you just one more thing?"

Amane didn't know what Asahi's question would be, so he was slightly on guard.

"Go ahead."

"…The girl, is she happy now?"

Asahi asked his question with the same, unchanging gentle expression. His tone of voice and the look in his eyes were pleading for his daughter's happiness.

Amane squeezed his hands into fists, then let out a slow sigh.

"…There's no way to know without asking her yourself. But I'm trying to make her happy. I'm confident that I can, and I'm going to do my best."

His words were full of aspiration, pride, and determination.

He never intended to part with that tenderhearted, dainty girl who hungered for love.

He wanted to make her smile always—and to be the one to make her happy. He was determined to do just that. No matter what anyone else said, he didn't intend to waver from that purpose.

When Amane stated his intentions clearly in a firm, even voice, the caramel-colored eyes across the table opened wide, then, in the next moment, softened in unmistakable relief.

"I see. I'm glad to hear it."

Something about Asahi's soft smile reminded Amane of Mahiru.

"...It isn't my right to ask this of you, but please take care of her."

"I'm going to make her happy, whether you ask me to or not."

"I see... Thank you."

Even though Amane probably deserved to be scolded for his tone of voice and rude attitude, Asahi smiled happily at him.

Through a haze of complicated feelings, Amane replied, in a voice that was just a little less prickly than before, "There's no reason for you to thank me."

When Amane returned home after parting ways with Asahi, Mahiru was quietly sitting on the sofa.

Ordinarily, when she was at his place, she came to the door to greet him when he got home. But on that day, she didn't seem able to move.

Mahiru projected tranquility with a hint of discomfort. She didn't seem calm exactly, more like she had forced herself to settle down. She turned to look at Amane, without moderating her expression at all.

"I talked to him," he said.

"Did you?"

Her slightly chilly tone was probably the result of an attempt to stay as composed as possible.

In response, Amane looked at her as gently as he could and quietly took a seat beside her.

As soon as he was settled next to Mahiru, she gently leaned over and snuggled up against him. It wasn't her usual sweet behavior. Instead, she gave Amane the impression that she was clinging to him for support.

...She must have been anxious.

She had been pretending like it was no big deal, but the father who had neglected her had made contact after all this time—and with her boyfriend no less.

Mahiru didn't seem to think that her father was such a terrible character, but she must have still been anxious about their meeting.

"There was nothing like what you seemed to be worried about... He was calm and quiet the whole time, more so than I had imagined."

"Oh, I see."

"...Should I tell you what we talked about?"

"Whatever you want. If you think it's best to tell me, then please do."

Even as she said she would leave it up to Amane, Mahiru seemed a little afraid to hear what he had to say. Amane squeezed her trembling hand.

He had decided he ought to go ahead and tell her.

He didn't fully understand what her father had been thinking when he had chosen to meet, not with his daughter, but with his daughter's boyfriend. But he felt he ought to at least let Mahiru know that her father had no intention of making her unhappy.

"I'm certain that Asahi doesn't intend to do anything to you. He told me that he's not planning to wreck your current life."

"...I'm glad to hear that."

"Then I asked why he wanted to see you, but he didn't tell me everything. Just that he wouldn't be able to see you anymore, so before that happened, he wanted to check on you one last time... That's the gist of what he said."

At Amane's words, Mahiru grumbled, "He never came to see me before now, so it's a little late for that."

But her voice seemed like it carried more bitterness than contempt.

"...This is just my impression," Amane continued hesitantly, "but when we met, Asahi seemed like he cared about you, Mahiru... He even seemed like he wanted you to be happy."

That was exactly why it was all so puzzling.

Why would Asahi wish for his daughter's happiness now? If he was going to regret it, he should never have neglected his child in the first place. If he had done that, Mahiru could have grown up without suffering such loneliness.

Mahiru sighed softly.

"...Honestly, I don't really understand my so-called parents at all."

Mahiru's voice was quiet, but it reached him as she continued. "They think they've fulfilled all the duties of child-rearing so long as they give me money. They're just strangers connected to me by blood. That's my impression of them."

In a detached tone, Mahiru told Amane how she really felt. Her expression was stiffer than usual and seemed to lack vitality.

"They never looked my way. No matter how good of a kid I was, they never saw me. Even when I reached out for them, they never took my hand... So it was only natural that I stopped reaching out. And that I stopped expecting anything from them."

Amane could tell that Mahiru had stopped expecting anything from her parents precisely because they had always ignored her before.

And he didn't think that her decision had been wrong. Though still a child, Mahiru had perceived that her parents didn't love her, and that she couldn't expect anything from them. It was inevitable that she had stopped hoping. It was her way of protecting herself.

"...I've always known that my father was capable at his job and that he had a good personality. Even so, that doesn't change the fact that he never looked my way, so I'm not sure how I should view him. At this point, I don't know how I should react to his attention."

"Mm."

"...Really, why now?"

"Mm."

"If he'd come to me earlier, I—"

Mahiru's sentence trailed off.

Instead, Amane heard a shaky exhalation as she quickly closed her mouth.

Her tightly sealed lips were trembling terribly, perhaps because she was squeezing them together so hard, and she was blinking a lot. Her eyes were watering like she was about to cry, but no tears spilled over. She just looked like she was trying to quietly weather the storm raging inside her.

Her ephemeral figure looked like it might dissolve and disappear. Amane embraced her and turned her face into his chest.

As he had done before when she had encountered her mother, he covered her up with a blanket.

Even though there wasn't much to hide this time, Amane wrapped her up entirely and held her close.

Her delicate body trembled in his arms, but he didn't hear any sobbing.

Still, she didn't seem ready to lift her head. She surrendered herself to Amane just like that and buried her face into his chest.

When she looked up again, the area around her eyes wasn't red. Perhaps she had calmed down a little while Amane held her. Her eyes themselves were wavering a little bit, but she didn't seem hopelessly distressed.

"...Mahiru, what do you want to do?"

Amane waited until after she had calmed down to ask the question.

Mahiru cast her eyes downward. "...I don't know," she replied. "I just—I like things the way they are now. Even though he finally showed up, I can't properly acknowledge that man as a parent."

"Gotcha."

©Hanekoto

"...I wonder if that's wrong for me to say, as his daughter?"

"The answer to that depends on your viewpoint, so I can't say for certain. But I don't think it's strange of you to think that way, and I won't deny your right to do so. If that's how you feel, I think that's fine. I accept your view and your choices."

"...Okay."

Whether she was wrong wasn't for Amane to determine.

Personally, he didn't think it was strange that Mahiru didn't recognize her parents as parents anymore. They had never done anything parental and had never accepted her affection, so it was impossible for her to see them that way.

"I'll be there for you, whatever you choose. I'm still an outsider, so I can't get too involved in your family affairs. But I respect your opinion, and I'll support you no matter what."

"...Sure."

"I'll always be by your side. If you ever feel anxious, you can lean on me."

Amane had already made up his mind about that.

He had no intention of ever letting Mahiru go. He was going to live the rest of his life cuddled up close to her.

In the past, he had heard from his parents' friends that the people of the Fujimiya family were excessively affectionate. He knew he was no exception.

Amane smiled a little.

He was convinced he would absolutely never lose the feelings he had for Mahiru.

That wasn't a prediction, it was a conviction.

He had always had a tendency to like one thing and stick with it, and that wasn't likely to change now that the object of his affection was a person.

His beloved girlfriend scrunched up her face at Amane's words, then she wrapped her arms around him, as if to say she wouldn't let him go.

"...You'll really stay by my side?" she asked.

"Of course."

"...So if I said I don't want to go home or be alone... If I said that, would you accept it and let me stay, Amane?" she said in a gloomy whisper.

Amane answered without hesitation, "Do you even need to ask?

"If it's what you want," he continued, "I'll stay by your side forever. I'll never leave you... Do you want to try staying over, to test it out?"

He asked the question in a deliberately teasing tone, and Mahiru, who seemed to understand the meaning behind his words, instantly went from looking like she might cry to blushing bright red.

Amane knew exactly what he was saying, so he also felt embarrassed, but when he saw how Mahiru's eyes darted around and how she was frozen stiff with bashfulness, he felt more in control.

"...You don't have to worry; you'll never be alone again."

He whispered the words softly, trying to calm the pounding of his heart. Mahiru's eyes filled with tears for a different reason than they had earlier, and she nodded.

Afterword

Thank you very much for picking up this book.

My name is Saekisan, and I am the author. I trust you enjoyed Volume 6 of *The Angel Next Door Spoils Me Rotten*.

The previous volume was a collection of short vignettes, but with this volume, we've returned to the main storyline. There's still plenty of summer vacation left!

Here we see Amane, sorting out ties from his past, one by one, while flirting at his parents' house, and Mahiru, reflecting on her own past while she watches him. The two of them have a similar temperament, but in some ways their upbringings were exactly opposite, so I hope you will bear that in mind as the story moves along.

But anyway, after going through this and that, Amane is growing up all right, so he might just have the capacity to care for all of Mahiru's needs and make her smile and be happy, don't you think? Even as the author, I can see that he's really changed compared to the first book. Who could have predicted he would become such a romantic young man?

In addition to Amane and Mahiru, I also touched briefly on Itsuki's and Chitose's circumstances, in a continuation of the last volume. The two of them have various problems of their own, and I plan to come back to their story again in future installments.

Once again, I was fortunate enough to have Hanekoto draw the wonderful illustrations for this volume. As always, the only way I can describe them is "wonderful."

Since Volume 6 is a continuation of the characters' summer vacation, I got Hanekoto to put Mahiru in her *yukata* on the cover. She is an extremely polished and beautiful young lady. I'm terribly jealous of Amane, who gets to accompany such a beauty.

Once again, there is an angel's feather hidden on the cover, so try to find it, everyone!

Also, the frontispiece showing Amane and Mahiru sleeping together is just tremendous. Somehow, even though hardly any skin is exposed, it's still really ero—(the sentence abruptly breaks off here).

Wholesome! We're keeping everything wholesome! There's no way that a loser—I mean, a gentleman—like Amane could ever do anything naughty! But even as I say that, there's only so far a person can be pushed, so I'm looking forward to seeing how long Amane can hold out (as if that's somebody else's problem).

Well then, here we are at the end, and it's time for me to thank everyone to whom I am so obliged.

To the head editors who put so much effort into getting this series published, to everyone in the editing department at GA Books, to everyone in the sales department, to the proofreaders, to Hanekoto, to everyone at the printing press, and to all of you who picked up a copy of this book, I am truly grateful.

Let's meet again in the next volume.

Thank you very much for reading all the way to the end!

©Hanekoto

Author
Saekisan

An author of romantic comedies whose staple diet is stories about mutual pining.

Mutual love is good, too.

With each passing volume, grows more convinced that being lovey-dovey is the way to go.

Both mutual love and mutual pining are great!

Illustrator
Hanekoto

A freelance illustrator living in Hokkaido.

Has always loved the *okonomiyaki* and chocolate bananas you can buy at festival stalls.

Tried to arrange the shape of Mahiru's gauze obi to look a little like wings.

HAVE YOU BEEN TURNED ON TO LIGHT NOVELS YET?

86—EIGHTY-SIX, VOL. 1–12

In truth, there is no such thing as a bloodless war. Beyond the fortified walls protecting the eighty-five Republic Sectors lies the "nonexistent" Eighty-Sixth Sector. The young men and women of this forsaken land are branded the Eighty-Six and, stripped of their humanity, pilot "unmanned" weapons into battle...

Manga adaptation available now!

WOLF & PARCHMENT, VOL. 1–7

The young man Col dreams of one day joining the holy clergy and departs on a journey from the bathhouse, Spice and Wolf. Winfiel Kingdom's prince has invited him to help correct the sins of the Church. But as his travels begin, Col discovers in his luggage a young girl with a wolf's ears and tail named Myuri, who stowed away for the ride!

Manga adaptation available now!

SOLO LEVELING, VOL. 1–8

E-rank hunter Jinwoo Sung has no money, no talent, and no prospects to speak of—and apparently, no luck, either! When he enters a hidden double dungeon one fateful day, he's abandoned by his party and left to die at the hands of some of the most horrific monsters he's ever encountered.

Comic adaptation available now!

THE SAGA OF TANYA THE EVIL, VOL. 1-12

Reborn as a destitute orphaned girl with nothing to her name but memories of a previous life, Tanya will do whatever it takes to survive, even if it means living life behind the barrel of a gun!

Manga adaptation available now!

SO I'M A SPIDER, SO WHAT?, VOL. 1-16

I used to be a normal high school girl, but in the blink of an eye, I woke up in a place I've never seen before and—and I was reborn as a spider?!

Manga adaptation available now!

OVERLORD, VOL. 1-16

When Momonga logs in one last time just to be there when the servers go dark, something happens—and suddenly, fantasy is reality. A rogues' gallery of fanatically devoted NPCs is ready to obey his every order, but the world Momonga now inhabits is not the one he remembers.

Manga adaptation available now!

VISIT YENPRESS.COM TO CHECK OUT ALL OUR TITLES AND. . .

GET YOUR YEN ON!